Variations of Jade

Perfect Love Wrong Time

Mable Rechee' Prunty

Copyright © 2021 Mable R. Prunty All rights reserved. ISBN: 9781792853821

Disclaimer

This book is a work of fiction. Names, characters, places, and incidents either are the products of the Author's imagination or are used fictitiously. Any resemblance to actual events, locales, or persons, living or dead, is entirely coincidental. Absolutely, no part of this publication is allowed to be reproduced, stored in a retrieval system, or transmitted in any form. Electronic, mechanical, audio, or photocopying Without written notarized permission from the Author-Mable Rechee' Prunty.

Variations of Jade

Perfect Love Wrong Time

v

Part I

If looks Could Kill

Small Town Changes

Ready for School

Strategic Klutz

Level Up

Quincy's Side of The Tracks

Don't let Nobody Control your Emotions

Aiden

Quincy

Daphne

Always Secure your spot

Perfect Love, Wrong Time

Meet me at the Pond

Missing Love

Fluffy Cotton and Waterfalls

Earline-RN

Go Time

Never Look Back

Part II

Vanessa's Breath of Fresh Air

Nervous Wreck

Richard-Finding the lost Spark

A Go or No

Thank You for Your Service

Permanent

Samantha and Byron

Some Vacation Day

Road Trip

Richard

Vanessa

Byron and Samantha's New Spark

Reunited

Part III

Meet Jade

Carol-New Town, Fresh Start

They After the Thomas Baby

Jade Goes to School

Adopted

Skate Time

Missing Pieces

Nichelle

Surprise Guest

Jade

Unanswered Questions

Daddy's Girl

Crush

The Grove

Definition of True Love

My Sweet Jade

Teens

Better Take a Test

Pen to Paper

--The END--

Variations of Jade Book Chat

Little Note from Author

Book Description

Variations of Jade

Perfect Love Wrong Time

Dedication

This book was written with little girls, young ladies, and women in mind who may be struggling with their past,

depression, identity, feelings of abandonment, and or low self-esteem. My hope would be for them to strive to be the best version of themselves daily. I would also hope they realize their past hurt, pain, or previous shortcomings do not define who they are or defeat which they have the potential to become. I pray they find their purpose and finally have the clarity to recognize their worth without seeking validation from anyone else.

Acknowledgments

First and foremost, I would like to thank God. Without him, none of this would be possible; therefore, I give him

all the praise. I would also like to thank my Momma, Daddy, and grandparents as a whole. They gave me a solid foundation to stand on, regardless of what I may have faced in my life.

Daddy, thanks so much for being a great example of a Husband and loyal friend. Your models were consistent and

placed before me at a young age. I always use those standards to measure others by as well as attempt to live by myself. I am forever a Daddy's girl!!

To my Momma, the late Earline Taylor, I miss you every day. You were my BFF and shoulder when I needed to be

vulnerable and transparent. Not a day goes by without me thinking of you. No matter how I try, there is nothing I can ever say that could sum up how much I love you or how grateful I am to have had the privilege of holding the title of your baby

girl.

To my Freshman English teacher. Thank you for encouraging me to write. Even when I felt awkward and unsure if

anything, I may have written was worth reading, you always took the extra time to encourage me and make me think that whatever I had inside was worthy of sharing with the World.

To my siblings, Nieces, Nephews, Cousins, Aunts, and My BFF's, thank you all for the love and support you gave

me and many, many years of happy memories and I love you all!!

To Jerome' (Sarah), KJ, Destini, Khloe,' Londyn, and Jayceon-My handsome grandson, you all have given me the

joy I needed daily to stay grounded. Just a simple smile or hug meant everything in the World to me most days. I thank God every day for loving me so much; He gave me you!

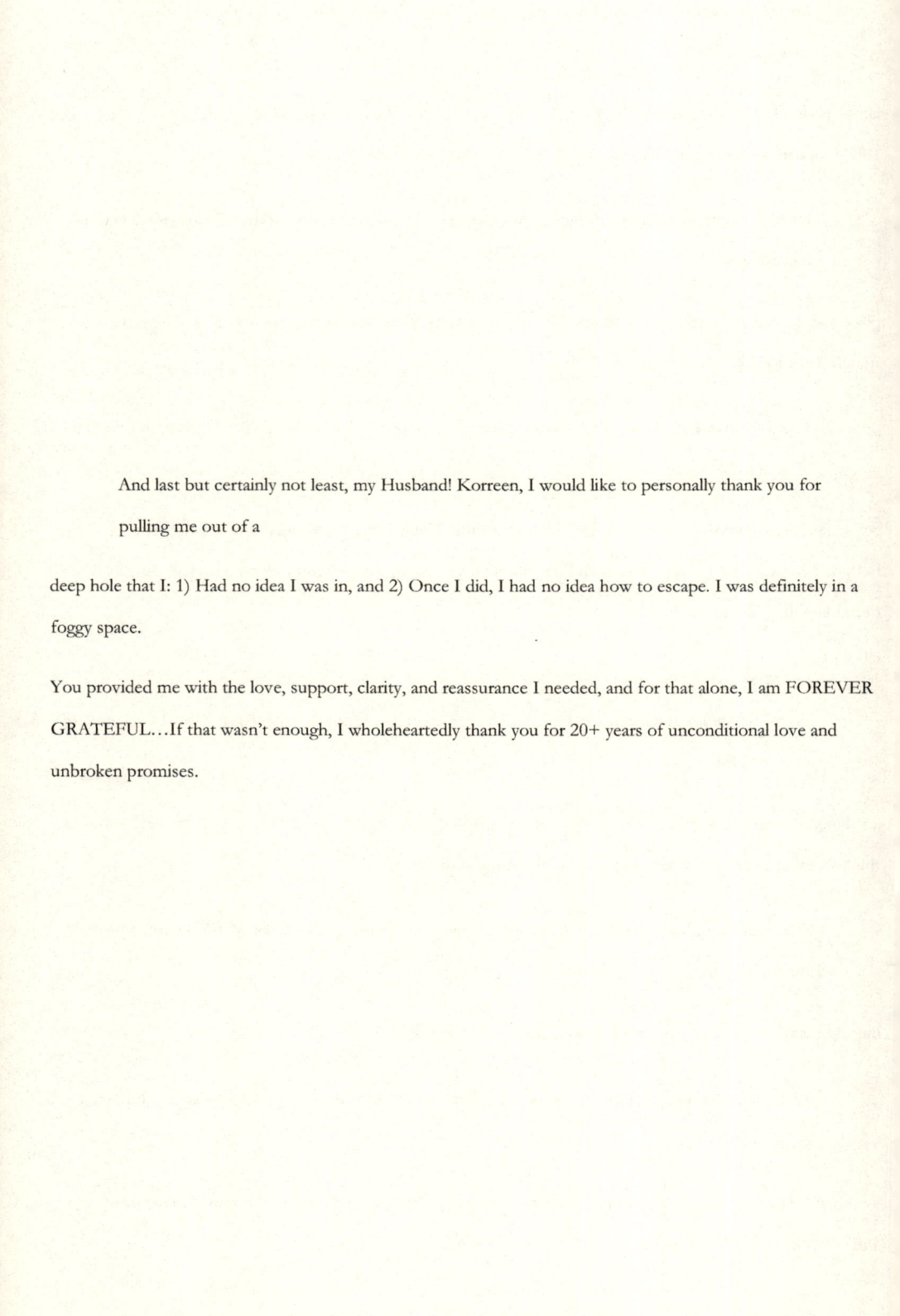

And last but certainly not least, my Husband! Korreen, I would like to personally thank you for pulling me out of a deep hole that I: 1) Had no idea I was in, and 2) Once I did, I had no idea how to escape. I was definitely in a foggy space.

You provided me with the love, support, clarity, and reassurance I needed, and for that alone, I am FOREVER GRATEFUL…If that wasn't enough, I wholeheartedly thank you for 20+ years of unconditional love and unbroken promises.

About the Author

Mable Rechee' Prunty APRN-BC is a lifelong resident of Jonesboro, Arkansas. She is a 2010 recipient of the

St.Bernards Medical Centers' Living the Mission Award and a 2018 finalist for the Healthcare Heroes award in Women's

Health. She has approximately Twenty years' experience in healthcare in various positions. Starting as a housekeeper, then a Patient care Technician, RN, then graduated in 2013 as a Board Certified APRN. She applied to and was 1 of 5 students accepted into the 2016 ASU Nursing Doctoral program. At the same time, her current career was starting to unfold, so she decided to place that on hold to be the best provider she could be without any distractions. Currently, she is a full-time provider at a pregnancy clinic. Alongside her close friend/Cohort, they were able to open the clinic in 2016 due to the vision they had to provide care to patients who did not have options for their care given their financial hardships and lack of insurance. There she can provide care to those individuals and be a listening ear to issues they may face physically and personally. Throughout this process, she has obtained her patients' and co-workers' trust and made many lifelong relationships.

As a child, she had a vast imagination and often wrote short stories. It has always been one of her lifelong dreams to become an author. It wasn't until she was in college that her English instructor gave her the confidence to pursue her dream after reading one of her short stories. Of course, life happened, and the goal was on the back burner for some time.

Over the years, Mable has consistently made every attempt to defy the odds. She makes it a point to tackle adversity head-on and persevere through whatever obstacle she may face. Her motto is, "If you have a desire in your heart, it was placed there by God for you to achieve it." She is a wife, a mother of 4; 2 sons and two daughters. She also has a daughter-in-law and a very handsome grandson. She lives in her hometown with her Husband and their two younger daughters.

Part I

If Looks Could kill

One of the floor's charge nurse responsibilities on the Labor and Delivery unit at Christine Baker Community

Hospital was to help return babies to the Mothers' rooms after Pediatricians did their morning exams. On a frigid day in December 1975, when the Charge nurse entered room 813, a 16-year-old girl sat. Very frail, and even in complete darkness, still, very noticeably pale.

It took every ounce of energy Daphne had left to sit up in bed when the door opened. When the nurse entered, she

slowly pushed an old metal bassinet into the room and placed it near the bedside. The nurse then looked down at Daphne with a look of pity and disappointment, never said a word, just walked out and closed the door behind her. For anybody else, the look she gave, or lack of conversation may sting a bit, but Daphne was so numb to both by now. Plus, that was the least of her worries at this point.

There she sat, all alone in the darkroom with a little person who had changed her World entirely. For the last nine

months, Daphne had lived an emotional roller coaster of a life. Although awaited with some excitement, this day will also be one of the most challenging days yet. Against her better judgment, Daphne glanced over at the bassinet but could only see the tip of what looked to be a pink blanket. It's a girl, she thought. She didn't know the sex until then. Maybe they did tell her earlier but seeing as how she was in a slight state of shock, the only way to mentally manage the day's events was to tune everybody out.

The second the door closed, her initial instinct was to run over to the baby and pick her up. She slowly stood up to

reach for the edge of the pink, ruffled blanket. But as quickly as her burst of excitement came, she caught herself mid-stride, turned around, and slumped back down in bed. Tired mentally, physically, every muscle in her body hurt, and her bottom felt three to four times its average size. If that wasn't enough, she's sixteen years old, alone, and just delivered her first child without any support, other than the Dr. and nurse who had to be there.

Just the mental reenactment of the day's events made the tears began to flow. Those same tears that had run freely

for months now. In all honesty, they have almost been a daily staple. Daphne and the little person she's provided food and oxygen for conveniently now share the same space. Her best listening ear when she needed it and a soul to count on when she felt all alone. However, even though only two to three feet exist between them, it may as well be a mile because she still couldn't take it upon herself to touch her, much less look at her.

Small Town Changes

All over the World, race inequality had been an issue for some time. Even here several discussions happened in an

attempt to improve things. It was a small step, but there was still a lot of work to do, and I think everybody knew things would not improve overnight. However, in August 1972, in Bronsonville Heights, the small community made preparations to integrate our Schools. Worldwide, a large number of Schools had been integrated for some time now, but it had just been a discussion here a couple of years before that.

Bronsonville Heights was a Rural, farming town, but a nice place to stay overall. Population right at ten-thousand,

but everybody was pretty much on a first-name basis. That didn't change the fact that the African American population still faced issues here from time to time. Issues blacks in larger, more diverse areas may not face near as often. Some of the residents here wanted our part of the town to remain separate in a way and it kind of always had been. Even though it's all called Bronsonville Heights, railroad tracks separated the black families from the white families for as long as I can remember.

But times were changing faster than some people wanted it to and wanted our Town to remain in a permanent

bubble. Of course, that would never happen, but I will say, as a result of their mindset, the changes set in place as a result of the Civil Rights Movement took longer to implement in this small, town.

Our family was a close-knit, hardworking family. Momma sewed from home, and Daddy worked on Wimbleton Farm, sometimes sixty to seventy hours a week during peak harvest. He had worked there for the last twenty years. He often said they treated him ok, but he didn't feel secure there even to this day. He talked about how Mr. Wimbleton wasn't a nice man. Immensely wealthy, but condescending, privileged, and arrogant. He said he always felt like he was walking on eggshells when Mr. Wimbleton was around. He had hope that when his son Aiden Wimbleton grew up, he would run things differently. But he now knew that would be the farthest thing from the truth. Over the last year or so, he realized he is already worse than Old man Wimbleton, which says a lot since he's only a year or so older than me.

Even with all the hard work and pinching pennies, we had had issues making ends meet from time to time.
Sure, we

always had lights, and we never went a day without food, but I sure didn't grow up with a silver spoon in my mouth or nowhere near it. Plus, if money makes you act like the Wimbletons, then I'd rather not have any.

Momma said many times, the love a family has for one another is worth more than any amount of money and I can't help but agree. I loved my family, and I grew up knowing they loved me. I especially loved the relationship me and

Momma had. She always told me I was a "Change of life baby," which may have meant to most they were unwanted. But not me. I knew without a doubt when she told the story about when she found out she was pregnant with me, and or when I was born, I knew I was special and wanted from the very beginning.

Without a doubt, my parents were visibly older than most of my friends' parents, but it never really bothered
me. I

felt blessed to have them because they instilled in me from the beginning how important family and loyalty for one another was. I knew whatever challenges I may face, they would be right there to walk me through them, as would I for them. Funny thing is, family values can be instilled in you from birth, but life events can overshadow everything you had been taught when a problematic situation is front and center at your doorstep.

Ready for School

I looked through my closet for weeks leading up to the first day of seventh grade. I'm sure I'm probably one of the only teens who actually enjoyed School. No, I was in no way looking forward to all the work but School for me meant a social life. As long as School was in, I wouldn't have to go a day without seeing my best friend, Christy. That's the main reason I hated Summer break. In the Summer, her Momma worked a lot, so Christy had to stay home and take care of her baby brother. Seeing as how we are only going to the seventh grade, she didn't think it was a good idea for me to come over when she wasn't home. She knew how excited we were when we got together and thought we would get distracted, and something could happen to the baby. We still talked on the phone from time to time, but of course, that wasn't the same.

I only hope we can be in some or all of the same classes. We've been friends since the first grade and pretty much as close as sisters; Especially since she only has a younger Brother and my Brother and Sister have been out of the house since I was like 5 or 6. This year is even more exciting because were moving to a new School and High School at that!! We're not going far since it's still on the campus of our old School but its brand new and we will stay there until we graduate. It's a big deal because it makes us feel like we're moving up in the World and not babies anymore.

Since the law was passed, all the students in the area had to go to the same School, our old one wasn't big enough, so they had to build another School for us older kids. Before the new one, we all went to the same School from Kindergarten to twelfth grade. Over Summer break, leading up to this School year, I heard Momma and Daddy talking about it a lot. Then, a few times, Momma was even on the phone with Christy's' Momma talking about it too. I don't know why, but they would lower their voice or change the subject when I came into the room. I know I'm only going to the 7th grade, but I'm smart enough to realize some people aren't happy about us all going to School together. I don't see what the big deal is. I think it's neat that we will be able to meet new people this year.

Strategic Klutz

Even-though the talk about the new kids coming was such a big deal before School started, everything actually went pretty smooth. There really hadn't been any huge issues. Sure, there were some people mouthing and a couple small fights initially, but after a couple months, all that kind of stopped. I know there were a lot of kids who still didn't want them here, though. I can tell by the snide looks and refusal to acknowledge them at times. Aiden Wimbleton was the World's worst. He had a group of friends, or should I say followers, who caused issues initially, and even though there hasn't been a lot of activity from them lately, you never know what he has up his sleeves because he's capable of doing just about anything. Throw the rock and hide his hand type.

Even if he didn't hide his hand, his Daddy would make sure whatever it was, would disappear.

I said I loved School, but I actually hated PE class. Partly because I was very uncoordinated. I would have much rather have been writing or reading a good book in a corner somewhere. Rather than dressed out with a Gym full of boys. They could be so annoying. In typical boy fashion they always had to try and be complete show-offs, which for me was a complete turn off.

Quincy was one of the star players on the Schools' Varsity basketball team. That's saying a lot since he's only in the seventh grade. He was one of the Black students who came when we merged the Schools. I had a couple classes with him, and he was always quiet. Then I saw him off and on in the halls or lunch since the beginning of the School year, and he never said much then either. But it's the end of the School year, and we have PE together. I can see that he turns into a completely different person anytime he has his hands on a basketball. He was far from quiet; he even yelled at some other players when they weren't taking the game seriously. That's really the only activity I felt he was ever interested in while we were in PE.

Then one day, at the end of class, me and Christy were standing around talking, and if I hadn't ducked when I did, his basketball would have hit me directly in my face. At first, I looked at him like he was such a klutz, then once he was close enough to grab his ball and apologize, I had to look away. His eyes were so beautiful and could draw you in. Then, his shy smile was contagious and genuine. The minute he apologized and asked me if I was ok, everything changed. From then on, he had my undivided attention. I had never been so happy that I had almost been smacked in the face with a basketball.

Ironically, PE, which had been my most dreaded class, in than instant became my favorite subject.

After that day, we became friends. Secretly, though, since a few people still have some issues with them, especially Quincy, he was a starting player on the Varsity team. Some people thought he didn't deserve the spot since he just got here. Then, I heard a couple guys on the team say they may have, had that spot if he would have never come. Over the next year or so, one thing led to another, and as they say, the rest was history. The only person who knew
about our relationship was Christy. There was no way I wouldn't have told her. We had been best friends for as long as I could remember, and we had always been able to tell each other everything. At first, she thought it was a little weird, me dating a black guy, but the more she was around him, the more she realized how "normal he was," she really didn't see any difference. She even helped us meet up a lot. I would tell Momma I was

going to her house on the weekends, and I would, but now that her brother stayed with their Daddy, and her Momma had a new boyfriend, she was okay with me staying. She would stay with him most weekends, and she didn't want Christy to be home by herself, so she actually felt better with me being there.

They had a big older house that had a huge basement. That's pretty much where we spent time together. Quincy, or as I called him, "QT," would come by after basketball practice most Fridays. Which was pretty much the only time we would be able to sit and talk for hours. Plus, it was a safe place for us to truly show our affection for one another. He was such a gentleman, and that was one of the things I loved about him. Even with all the alone time we had, he never pressured me into doing anything. For the first couple of years, all we really did was talked about our goals, dreams, held hands, and much later kissed.

Of course, I didn't tell my parents about our friendship. Quincy, on the other hand, did tell his. He said he had always tried not to keep secrets or lie to them. He was always told they could work through anything as long as he was honest with them. Even after he told them about our friendship, I would see his Momma at some of the games, and she would always make it a point to smile and speak to me. That made me feel like she really was okay with us being friends. He said he thought they were ok with it, partly because they had been so worried about him going to the new School initially, that us being friends made them breathe a little better about him being there.

Even-though his family seemed somewhat ok with us being friends, all understanding went out of the window when he told them about our relationship. Everything changed in a heartbeat. They were completely against it. He said his Daddy and Grandmother were both against him dating outside his race because they thought something would happen to him. He said they weren't racist at all, but they knew how things were, and that would be frowned upon and cause problems. He said he knew his Grandmother would have an issue with it, but he still wanted to tell her. He absolutely adored her and couldn't stand to keep anything away from her. He said even in the beginning, when they were just friends, she had always told him,

"boy, you are going to mess around and get killed messing with that girl!"

His Momma, on the other hand, was still ok with it, I think. He never really said anything she said, and I know they are really close. She was such a beautiful lady. Caramel skin tone, big bright brown eyes, a pretty smile, petite, and always dressed really well. Quincy had the same skin tone as her, and they have those same bright brown eyes.

Quincy thought he and his Momma were so close because he was her only child, and with his Daddy working away a lot, she poured her all into him. He was her best friend in a way and joked that he wished she could love him just a little less because her whole focus in life was on him. Even-though his Daddy had worked away overnight a lot, he was the more stern parent. Quincy had a lot of respect for both his parents and had always done what they asked. Our relationship was the first time he had ever defied them.

We believed our love from the beginning. For years we talked about our plans to get married when we turned 18. We would have to move to make that happen because I know our families would disapprove. He said I'm the first white girl that ever-showed interest in him, and I'm the only girl he's been drawn to. I guess I could say the same about him. Actually, he's the first black guy I had ever talked to. He said when he saw me, he liked me from the beginning. He tried to ignore the feelings initially because he had no idea, I even knew who he was or if I would date outside my race. He said he couldn't tell anybody but his Momma. Then at night, when he lay down, I was all he could think about. He may never admit it but, all that made me feel the whole basketball mishap was planned.

The first time he knew he had to act on his feelings was when he saw me at the other end of the court talking to a friend. Who he now knows was Christy. He said he stared at me so long that Coach Smith walked over and asked him what he was looking at. Quincy said he was able to make up a quick response; he told him he was trying to figure out what the School was having for lunch. Said his family was low on cash and he didn't have anything for dinner the night before. He said the coach gave him the "poor black kid look," but it worked. He walked away and never asked him again. Which allowed him to continue to sneak a peek every now and then.

We were so much alike that we never really had a big argument or anything. The most we had was a disagreement about a party he was invited to that I didn't want him to go to. He had been invited by some other guys on the team. Christy had told me she heard some guys saying they were going to try and get him drunk and let Coach know so he would be kicked off the team, which would mean he would be disqualified from the State Tournament. We had never been to State, plus I knew how hard he worked to single-handedly get us there. I didn't want to hurt his feelings, but I didn't want him to go to the party and get set up either. Finally, I had to break it to him that it was a rumor out that something was supposed to happen there. He only wanted to go so the guys wouldn't be offended. Once he heard that, he decided to stay home Afterall.

Level Up

One day, while sitting in class, I decided it was time for us to take our relationship to the next level. I realized how hard this was on both of us, and I knew it was time for us to connect the way we both wanted to. I had thought about it for months before I decided, but the final decision came to me one day in English class. Believe it or not, it was the only class we had together since the PE class we had a little over two years ago. I glanced up during a writing assignment and saw how Toya Roberts was looking at Quincy. After class, I could almost read her mind, and I saw her grab his hand and smile when he walked by her desk. I could tell he wasn't interested, but she was persistent, and let's just say, her reputation wasn't the best. She pretty much got whatever it was she wanted, and it looked as if he was next on her list.

I couldn't be mad at her; she had no idea we were together, and I mean, he was a good catch, so I can't blame her for trying to put her hooks in him. Quincy told me not to worry. He said he had no interest in somebody throwing themselves off on him. I get it, but how long can a guy pass up something that's thrown in his face? Then she was his same race. I knew, even with her flaws, his family would much more approve he date her over me. That played heavy on my mind and heart. I could never be for him what Toya could be. I would never be able to share stories about sharing the same struggles they have faced over the years. Or know everything about their culture, just yet. But I was willing to learn. What I was not going to do was lose him to her. That pretty much sealed the deal for me. I made up my mind, then and there, that it was time, and I was determined to take this thing a step further.

I loved him, and I knew he loved me, so there was no real reason to hold back. Of course, QT had no idea what I had in mind. I passed him a note that said basement, which was our code to meet up. Christy's Momma had to work overnight, and Momma and Daddy had to go out of town to handle some business. Plus, Christy and Aiden had plans to go to the movies. Which meant we would have the place to ourselves. It was a perfect situation in my eyes until Christy reminded me it probably wouldn't look good if she was out and I wasn't with her. Maybe somebody would see her, and then it could get back to Momma that I wasn't with her at the Movies. I agreed, so we all changed our plans last minute. Christy said instead of going to the movies, she and Aiden would stay home. She was excited since this was to be the first time they could have some alone time. Since he didn't know about me and Quincy, we decided to head over to the Pond and give them some privacy. The Pond was our other place. It was dark, and nobody was ever there at night because woods and brush surround it. But in our eyes, it's gorgeous because we have a lot of memories there. Then, even though it's unkempt and dark, some distant lights make a reflection on the water. The sparking reflection always made me and Quincy feel like fireflies were dancing to the beat of our love, and it was beautiful.

Also, at this particular place, we would talk for hours, and the whole time he would lay beside me and stroke my hair. We talked about our goals; how he wanted to be a mechanic who would work on people's cars who couldn't afford the regular shops. He said he would work with them and make it easy for them to have running vehicles to get their families around and not rely on public transportation. I told him all I've ever wanted to do was be a wife and a Momma. He smiled and said he knew I would be great at both. It was stuff as simple as that. He was my one little piece of joy, and I loved everything about him. He was six feet tall but nothing more than a gentle giant. His skin was smooth as silk, and he had the perfect smile and the happiest laugh I ever heard. He had the best personality and was loved by pretty much everybody. Including me. If all that wasn't enough, I equally loved the way he smelled, touched me, treated me, but most importantly, the way he made me feel. He made me feel so special, like I had a purpose in life; when he looked at me, he was looking at ME!! When he spoke to me, he talked to me and waited for my response as if what I had to say was the most crucial thing in the whole wide world. Even-though our conversation was innocent, the love I had for him made my body yearn for us to connect finally, and I knew by the way he looked and touched me, he felt the same way.

That night, once we knew Aiden had left, we headed back to Christy's. When we made it to the house, we went in through the basement. I told him I would run upstairs to let her know we were back. I chatted with her a little bit about her, and Aiden then headed to the bathroom to freshen up. I used some of her Mommas' perfume and lathered my entire body down in some of her expensive lotions. I put on my black pajama set, headed back downstairs, and sat by him on the couch.

Still, Quincy didn't try anything. He complimented me on how nice I looked and smelled, but that was it. We laid on the floor and watched TV like we always did, but I started to massage his shoulders this time. I had no idea what I was doing, but I had seen it on one of Momma's soap operas. At first, he was frozen stiff and never said anything, which made me kind of embarrassed. After a couple of minutes, he turned towards me and started kissing my neck, making the hairs stand up on my arms. Then, he pulled away abruptly and stood up. He said it was getting late, so he walked towards the window to make sure the coast was clear for him to leave. I knew he made that up because he told me earlier, he didn't have to be home until eleven, and it was just a little after eight.

I walked up behind him and put my hands under his shirt. I slid my fingers down his tight chest, through the tight hairs on his stomach, and rested them on the rim of his basketball shorts. I leaned into him and laid my head on his back. I could feel him breathing faster than usual and almost thought I could hear his chest pounding. He grabbed my hands and held them in his. He turned around and looked at me like he hadn't in the past. His eyes almost looked like they were begging me to stop but asking me to keep going at the same time. I could tell how difficult this was for him. He pulled away, but his body was responding, and there was no turning back. That cold February night, we kept each other warm by taking our relationship to a whole different level.

Quincy's Side of The Tracks

This year we had to go to School on the other side of the tracks. I sure didn't want to. I was finally about to head

over to the big kid School where I could be on the varsity basketball team. Then I would stay there until graduation. Then, my Momma, Daddy, and everybody I know went to our old School. Daddy played basketball and had tons of awards hanging up in the gym. I used to see them when we went to any of the Schools' basketball games. It made me feel proud to see my Daddy's name up there. I couldn't wait to try and beat his records when I started playing. That was a little competition we had planned for, for years. Now, there is no way my name could ever be by his since we had to go to the other School. My Daddy and Grandmother didn't want me to. They kept holding out hope that we wouldn't have to until they realized we did. But Momma said she was fine with me going because she thought it was a better opportunity. Mainly because our School didn't even have enough books to go around. I don't know why she was even worried about that because I've made straight A's my whole life.

She also thought I would also be able to get more exposure playing basketball there. All of that made sense, but she

still had her fears. The main thing she worried about was me being able to have a social life there. I had plenty of friends in my neighborhood that I went to School with my whole life and were all close. Most of them stayed at my house so much we fed them just about half their life. My Daddy mentored many of them because not too many families had a Momma and Daddy in the house. My friends teased me all the time and said my family was like the "Hawthorpes," which was one of the families on the soap operas all our Mommas watched.

I never had to go to the Principles office or anything, so she was worried I may have issues that could lead me there. The School was predominately white, which was different because nobody in my community had any dealings with anybody of the opposite race other than seeing them at one local store, hospital, or lite company. One thing we all always did was stayed on our side of the tracks. I never really knew why we did, I just know I had been taught that my whole life, so that's what I always did. But now I will have to go on the other side, which makes me feel a little funny. I know the laws and stuff have changed, and we got to go there, but I know some of the kids and teachers don't want us there. At my old School, all my teachers looked like me, and all made it a point to build us up, and I know they loved all of us and would help us in any way they could.

Momma, Daddy, and Grandmother went to a few meetings at our church about it a few times before the decision was made for us all to go there. Then one night, they had a meeting and wanted all of us kids to be there. So, a couple of weeks before School started, the whole community pretty much met up there. We all had to come to sit around, listen to the community's elderly members, talk about things they went through on the other side of the tracks, years ago. They spoke to us about the importance of not having any School issues by walking a straight and narrow path. Have respect for ourselves, the teachers, students, and the building. They wanted us to walk a straight and narrow path by trying to avoid or cause any problems. They said to stay out the folk's way and do what you are supposed to do, and you should be fine.

Everybody looked up to my Grandmother, and she spoke there as well. She specifically talked to us, the young men of the community. Her main thing was talking about the importance of staying away from the white girls at School. She said she wasn't prejudiced at all; she knows the risks involved with that whole situation. She then told us about a childhood friend who was murdered by some white men in the community when she was younger. She said one white family lived in a neighborhood close to our side of the tracks. There had been no issues or anything for a couple of years. Then, she started being friends with a black girl. They were inseparable until the girl told her Daddy that she thought the little girl's brother had looked through her window one night. Nobody believed it, but even if he did, he should not have had to suffer the way he did.

She said they caught him one night walking, took him, beat him, and hung him up in one of the neighborhood trees over by the Pond. She said they even pinned a note to his shirt that said, "Keep your eyes and hands off our girls and stay on your side of the Tracks."

My Grandmother always talked to me about the dangers of going on the other side of the tracks, but I thought she was overreacting. That was an eye-opener. I could tell by the looks on my friends' faces that this was the first time any of us heard how the tracks separating Bronsonville Heights had even started. I love my Grandmother to death and, there's no way I'm doing anything to worry her. I just hope the rest of these guys and girls listen to the advice they gave us.

Don't let Nobody Control your Emotions

It's been a month since we all started School, and so far, everything's been going ok. Sometimes I think everybody's

treating us nice for now, until the newness wears off and everybody stops watching. In the beginning me and everybody was, on edge waiting for something big to happen. It was even some reporters outside the first couple of days with cameras. Then some of the men from our neighborhood came in the mornings and afternoons for the first couple of weeks. They didn't do anything; they just wanted to make sure we made it in and home from School without any problems.

Outside of a few small fights that probably would have even happened at any School, everything has been pretty chill. I'm not stupid, though, and I still got my guard up. I don't eat or drink anything from nobody, go to nobody's house, or ride in the car with anybody. My Grandmother made me promise her that before the first day of School. She said those things could turn into something big, so she would be able to sleep well at night if I kept my promise to her. Of course, I love my

Grandmother to death, so I will do whatever she asks me.

I know I aint had any real problems but, I'm not stupid either. I've heard a couple of my teammates tell racist jokes

that are not in the least bit funny to me. Then, I've listened to a few of them say little stuff under their breath from time to time, but I just ignore it. One thing my Momma taught me was never to let nobody else control my emotions. And my Daddy always said, a team can't win if it's divided, and I'm all about winning, so if they got a problem with me, then they are just going to have to deal with it some other way because I'm not down with loosing.

Aiden

This School year has been a complete waste of time. All these others at the School make me not even want to go. I can't stand to look at them, and it makes my stomach cringe just to know I have to breathe the same air as them. My Daddy tried his hardest to keep them out from over here. He's got a lot of friends who didn't want them there either. Between him and them, they have run this town for years. To stop them from coming, he and his friends pulled favors, blackmailed some, and paid off others. As I said, it worked until the Judge couldn't ignore the order to make the changes anymore. He said the people were breathing down his neck. Said his hands were tied, so now he had no choice but to make the ordered changes. Once Daddy, the Judge, and his friends realized it would happen, they met with some of us boys and told us how we needed to help keep an eye on our girls. They didn't say how but just said it was our responsibility. That was most of what they said, but when me and Daddy made it home, we had another talk. He filled me in on some stuff he and his friends did when they were younger. Said it kept the folks on the other side of the tracks until now. He said if we could make an example from one of them, the rest would go back over the tracks and never return. If they refuse to go to the School, the law won't apply, and they could go right back to their School, and things will go directly back to normal.

Quincy

There is this one girl then I had noticed a couple of times in class. I'm not sure why but I'm kind of intrigued by her. I haven't felt this way about a girl ever. There was this one time I liked a girl in the 5th grade at my School, and we called ourselves going together for like a week. Then we had to break up because her Mama says she couldn't have a boyfriend until she turned 16. But this girl, I'm not sure what it is about her. All I can think about is how my Grandmother has dared me to even look at a white girl before now, but every time I head into class, I try to sit where I can have at least a small view of her.

Her name is Daphne. She's on the shorter side, small build, with long, dark curly hair that she keeps in a ponytail most times.

Then there was this one time I walked in class behind her, and she smelled so good. She's always with this other girl named Christy. I have a couple more classes with Christy than I do her. One time, I started to ask Christy was her friend seeing anybody but chickened out.

I had waited all year for my class because it is in the gym, and I know we would be able to play basketball at some

point. Once I got dressed out and walked into the gym, I saw Daphne and Christy. My day had been made because you have to sit the whole time in the other classes and can't talk, but in PE class, you're kind of all over the place, and you don't have to stay seated and quiet the whole time. Which could mean I may have an opportunity to at least speak to her. For weeks, I thought about how I could start a conversation with her. I had almost given up on it, then one day I was playing around with a basketball at the end of class . I glanced over towards her and before I knew it somebody hit my hand in the ball flew directly toward her face. Thank God she ducked because that would not have been the best way to make a first impression by hitting her in the face with the basketball. I walked over to apologize and grab the ball. I looked at her, and her face looked like she was gone give me a piece of her mind. I was starting to get scared, but then, the closer I got, her look softened, I apologized, and she accepted it. We laughed about it, and that started our friendship.

I never met anybody as genuinely sweet as her. When I first came, I didn't know what to expect. But for some

reason, this girl does not act like the picture painted for me about the people on this side of Town. She treats me well, and Momma was happy about our friendship. That's our main thing she was so worried that I wouldn't have anybody to socialize with at the New School. She said she knew it would be easier if I had friends in my corner. We knew being friends should be ok, but we still played everything low-key while we were at School because some people may not have understood our friendship. We were still just friends for a year or so after that. Of course, I had feelings for and wanted more initially, but I didn't want to push. Because again, she was my friend, but just because she was ok with being friends with me didn't mean she wanted to be in a relationship with me.

One day we made up over her friend Christy's house and watched a couple of movies. It was something about her that day. She just looked and acted differently. It was almost like she was throwing hints that she was interested in being more than friends. I'll admit I was nervous. As I said, I never had a real girlfriend. All I could think about was how I feel for her and how my family feels about the situation. I didn't want to go against what they said, but I felt too far gone to turn back. Having to switch up so much to come here was a big deal. I didn't know anybody and did not want to leave my School. Yeah it was ancient, and the books were worn and missing pages, but it was all we knew. But I'm glad I did because Daphne is the best thing that ever happened to me. I can't wait until we can be together without having to hide our affection for one another.

A lot of times, we decided to go to the Pond. Outside of School, the Pond and Christy's house were the only two places we could meet up. I always liked the Pond. Mainly because, even though we could watch tv and hang out over Christy's, I got nervous every time. Partly because I had to sneak in and out of the house, on the other side of the tracks, and it aint no way if somebody saw me going in, or coming out of her house, that I could explain I was invited. I always felt like I was being followed or watched. When I went inside, I was still on edge, thinking Christy's Momma may come home or something.

The Pond was on my side of the tracks. It's not that far, but it still makes me feel a little more safe being closer to home. Plus, one of my friends' place is a street or so over; I always felt like I could at least make it to his spot if somebody got after me or something. I know I shouldn't even have to think about stuff like that, but it's been in my head my whole life. Me and Daphne decided as soon as we turn eighteen, we're getting married. We would have to move out of Town to do it because even though it's a couple of years away, we knew our families still wouldn't approve.

Daphne

I replayed that night over and over again in my head. Then every-time I saw Quincy, my heart would pound a thousand times a minute. He felt the same way because he acted more shy than usual when he saw me after that. He was my first, and I was his, so we didn't have anything to compare it to, but I know our experience was perfect for us.

Christy was so interested in hearing about me and Quincy. Since she had not had sex before, I think she used our relationship as her soap opera. She was mesmerized by us that I didn't mind all her questions, but she did make me nervous by asking me a couple of times if I were scared I would get pregnant. I told her no, which was the first and only time I ever lied to her. I was really scared about that at first. Then I felt terrible because Quincy had no idea it would happen that night, so he didn't have any protection. I thought out the whole thing except that part. But, thankfully, I had my period that next week. It only lasted a day and lite I didn't mind, I was so happy to see it. Of course, we had played around and said our baby girl would be beautiful, and if we had a boy, he would certainly be a basketball star and handsome like his Daddy, but no time soon. We both said we need to take better precautions in the future because we may not be so lucky next time.

A couple of weekends passed, and I decided to stay with Christy again. I knew I wouldn't be able to see Quincy since he had a basketball tournament all weekend, but I was still looking forward to hanging out with her. Christy, on the other hand, had made plans to have Aiden over. She and Aiden had been together for about six months, and she liked him. She said they hadn't had any alone time because he's always busy with his family farm or wrestling practice. They were finally able to make plans to see each other for a couple of hours because They canceled one of his matches. She said she is seriously thinking about taking things to the next level. She said he's such a sweet guy, been so patient with her, and all the girls want him. She thinks if she doesn't hurry up and give in, he may leave her for somebody else.

Who was I to tell her not to? I mean, she does like him, and they have been together for a while, but it's something

about him that never really sat right with me. He acts entitled. Then I can't help but think about everything my Daddy had said about him and his family over the years. Like I said earlier, his family has money, and I feel like he looks down on people like us. Christy, at times, jumps through hoops to make him happy. It's almost like she thinks he's doing her a favor by being with her. I hate she feels that way. She's always been such a beautiful person inside and out. I know she's my friend, but I think anybody that knows her would say she's the prize and he's the lucky one to have her on his arm. I know for a fact, there are a lot of guys who kill to be with her.

Of course, she's got blinders on and can only see Aiden.

Even though I secretly didn't care for Aiden, I still respected their relationship as long as he made her happy. I had

homework to get caught up on anyway, so I decided to hang out in the basement and give them some privacy. I didn't get far with my homework because I started watching T.V. until it was watching me.

I woke up and glanced at my watch, and it was 0118. I could never hear what was going on upstairs, but I figured by now

Aiden was gone, so I grabbed my book bag to head upstairs. By the time I made it to the third or fourth step, I felt

something grab my ankle. I fell backward and must have hit my head on the floor because the next thing I remember was waking up in a daze, and Aiden was on top of me!! I was petrified, confused, and anxious all the same time!!

> He was sweaty, rough, and his breath smelled like tobacco. After my initial shock, I tried to push him off me and

told him to stop. That didn't work, so I started begging him to stop. I had no idea where Christy was, and even though I didn't want this to happen, I wanted him to stop without me having to yell to her for help. I would have no idea how to explain it all because I didn't have any explanation myself. The last time I saw them, they were upstairs cuddled up on the couch. He was determined and strong. I knew it was a no-win for me, so I warned him, if he didn't stop, I would scream. He chuckled a devilish laugh and I felt something sharp against my throat. He said if I made a sound, he would slice my throat without a second thought and nobody would believe my spook loving ass anyway. He whispered he knew all about me and

Quincy, and if I said anything to anybody, he and his boys would string Quincy's ass up and not serve a day in jail because his Daddy was friends with the Judge. Then said he would make my Daddy's life a living hell by firing his broke ass and see to it that he never works another day in this town. Then, barked, if I even thought about yelling for Christy, he would have no choice but to get rid of both of us. Before I could do or say anything else, he called me a bitch, grabbed me by my hair, and slammed my head against the floor!

Always Secure Your Spot

I could hear what sounded like a secondhand ticking on a clock and water slowly dripping in the distance. I sensed I was in the room by myself, but I wasn't sure. I tried to open my eyes, but I couldn't. Maybe my eyes were swollen shut from crying. Maybe I could open them, but my mind wouldn't let me because of what I feared I might see when I did. I lay there for what felt like hours but could feel a small breeze of air come from under the other door in the basement that led outside. I feel like that's how Aiden got in and out earlier and realized I must have forgotten to lock it earlier. I slowly walked to the door and locked it. The room I once loved and spent countless hours with many great memories now smelled like must and mold. What once felt cozy and comfy now felt cold and terrifying.

When I finally got the nerve to head upstairs, I open the door to Christy's bedroom, and there she lay, sleeping peacefully—surrounded by stuffed animals, with pink and purple everywhere. She looked so peaceful, innocent, and clean!! Which is the complete opposite of me because I feel so dirty. I tiptoe in her bathroom, trying not to wake her up. I have no idea what I look like and don't want to scare her. Plus, what would I say happened?

I close the bathroom door behind me and slide down the door on the cold floor. In a way, the cold tiles on the floor comfort my sore body. I lay on my side in a fetal position and cried silently. All I want is for Quincy to be here with me. But is he even going to want me after this? Do I tell him? Will he just know? Will the rumors get out? Will some way this turn into my fault?

I filled the white clawfoot tub with hot water. I always liked this tub. When we were younger, Me and Christy played together in here for years. We would fill the tub with bubbles and play in there for hours. We would make our faces up with bubbles and blow them all over the place. We wouldn't get out until our fingers and toes were shriveled up like prunes, and we were made to get out. Generally, most of the water was on the floor, and we used all the towels in the cabinet to clean it up before we were caught. How dumb were we because her Momma would know since she would be the one to do laundry?

I'm sure she knew but never said anything. I'm sure she let it go and wrote it off to kids just being kids.

I let the tub fill as high as I could, stepped in, and it was so hot I almost stepped back out. In all honesty, the pain from the water took my mind off the pain and events from last night. It was the first time my mind was able to think about something else, and I was grateful. I stayed in the bathtub until the water was cold. I sat there almost in a catatonic state until I heard a knock on the door. I sat up quickly and yelled," I'm in here." First time I heard myself since last night. My voice sounded hoarse, and my throat was so dry it felt like I had been eating chalk. It was all I could do to get those words out. Christy went on to say that was fine and said she would use the other bathroom.

I slumped back down in the water with a sigh of relief. I put the washcloth between my legs, and to my surprise, I

was so swollen. I couldn't bear to look. All I knew without a doubt, my body felt nothing like I remembered. I did glance down at my legs, and bruises were everywhere. Some red, purple, and some that looked almost black. The back of my head was tender, and I had a horrible headache. My right elbow had a large cut on it and several scrapes to both my knees. I had a large scratch on my side, side and a sizeable blood-filled blister on the inside of my bottom lip. Ironically once, I put on my jeans and t-shirt, there were no visible marks I would have to explain only if I could cover the mental ones.

> I'll never forget the first time I saw Aiden after that night. It was the next week, me and Christy were headed to

lunch and he was standing at the end of the hall talking to some of his friends. I'm convinced he only has some because they are either 1.) Spoiled brats with money like him, 2.) Have no respect for girls, and they are all just alike, or 3.) He's threatened them in some way, and they have no choice.

> I wanted to stop in my tracks, turn and go the other way, but Christy wanted to talk to him. She ran towards him

and hugged him. Of course, the whole time they hugged, he looked at me with a smug grin. My skin felt like something was crawling all over me when he yelled at me and said Hi. I could have thrown up. My mind went right back to that night and everything he called me. It made me even sicker that Christy still pretty much worships the ground he walks on.

On any given day, my emotions were from one extreme to the next. I see Quincy, and my heart smiles. Get a glimpse of Aiden, hear Christy talk about him, or hear his voice, I'm a nervous wreck. Why can't he just quit School and take over the farm? I'm guessing I'm selfish because while that would make things so much easier for me, my poor Daddy would catch hell, I'm sure.

Then one day before lunch, I got sick. I felt shaky, sweaty, and dizzy. I made it to the bathroom and put some water on my face. I sat down on the wooden bench to get a grip. I'm guessing I need to eat something since I had an early dinner last night and no breakfast. I head to the cafeteria and grab some chili and crackers. I ate it in no time and felt better. But later, when I got home, my stomach was upset. Momma said the chili may have been too spicy and may have just soured on my stomach. I'm not sure what that meant, but it made sense. She thought I should lay down for a little while, which I did but not long after that, I felt a burning sensation in the back of my throat.

Momma gave me some chalky tasting medicine that helped, and I went to sleep super early, but they woke up way earlier than usual. I figured I should get ahead and work on the homework I didn't have the opportunity to do the night before. The minute I reached down to grab my book bag, I threw up everywhere. I hated that I threw up, but I felt so much better afterward. I cleaned up the mess, took a bath, finished my homework, and headed off to School, but there is NO WAY I'm ever eating the School chili anymore.

Perfect Love, Wrong Time

I know you love her, Quincy, but we love you, and I don't see anything good coming out of this. A few ladies from work said they heard you were friends with her. I could tell by the tone in their voice, they suspected more. Right now it's just a suspicion but it won't take long for them and other people to find out you're more than that. I've always had an open mind concerning Daphne, but now that it's being discussed at work and thinking about everything your Daddy and Grandmother have said over the years, it makes me nervous.

Quincy-Momma, it's not like that. I know everything will be ok. I know how to protect myself, and I would never put myself in a situation to get hurt or anything. I always know what to do. Everything you and Daddy have taught me over the years. Say yes sir, no sir, don't have my hands in my pocket, don't be in the wrong place at the wrong time, and comply if I'm ever stopped and questioned for any reason.

Momma: I know your right; we have always prepared you, but this is bigger than that. And for that reason, me and your Daddy have been talking, and we have decided to move.

Quincy: Huh? Move where? When?

Momma: We're going to move closer to my family in Atlanta in a couple of weeks.

Quincy: What?? That's a long way away!! What about Daphne? My basketball team? We were on our way to State, plus Coach said I got some people coming to see me play!

Momma: I know, Quincy, and we have all that figured out. We got enrolled in an excellent School with an outstanding athletic program. The coaches are very excited to have you, and next Season you are guaranteed to start. They even have some scouts looking at you now to offer a scholarship.

Quincy: Momma, I can't leave Daphne. I love her so much!!

Momma: I know you do, son, but we love you more than you could ever love her. I have no doubt she's a nice person, but YOUR, our number one priority. Plus, I know you hate to admit it, but you two may genuinely have, The Perfect Love, But Wrong Time. the world's, not ready for you and Daphne… Not yet.

The next few weeks fly by. Momma said three weeks but didn't give me a date. I've been seeing Daphne, but I could never bring myself to laugh and talk to her. I know she's wondering what's been going on with me, and the timing couldn't be more off. We finally took our relationship to the next level, now this. That night was perfect. I had no idea what I was doing, and she didn't either, but it was perfect for us. Enough for me to eat, sleep and breathe that night. I keep replaying it over and over in my mind. I wish I could talk to her and let her know what's going on, but Momma said she didn't want anybody to know we were leaving or when. She said she didn't want any last-minute issues, so she told me to just be prepared to leave at any time. The last thing I want is for Daphne to think I used her; Which would make our previous three years together out to be a lie. I know a lot of guys do that, but that was never my plan. I planned on marrying her. Now they want me to leave without even saying bye or telling her why and even though it's not my fault, I can't help but feel guilty.

Another week passed and I feel like the house is more and more empty every time I come home from School.

Momma and Daddy are even picking me up from School now. They aren't taking any chances of me meeting up with Daphne. I don't know if they think we would run away or what. Today, though, Daddy is in the car too. The drive home is pretty quiet. We just had the typical, how was School conversation and then silence. They didn't even talk much. When we made it home, I knew why? As soon as I walked in, it was obvious that the house was completely packed up. It was so much more stuff missing than when I went to School, furniture wise. I went to my room, and my bed was even gone.

I sat down on the only piece of furniture left, my old blue chair with my backpack still on my shoulder, my basketball resting on my knee, and looking at the floor. I prayed so hard that they would change their minds', but I know that's not happening now. Momma walked into the room behind me. I knew it was her because she always knocks right before she walks in.

Daddy, on the other hand, never knocked. I never even looked up. Just ask when we were leaving.

Momma: In the morning. Everything we need is packed, and your Daddy will come back next week and grab the rest. -My heart is tight, and my throat feels like it is swollen and shut at the same time. I'm a big guy and didn't want Momma to see me cry, so I held in all the air I could until I could compose myself enough to ask if I could at least write Daphne a letter?

Momma: Son, and how do you plan on getting it to her?

Quincy: I don't know, I just wish I could.

Momma: Son, let's just make a clean break. Move on with your life. It will hurt in the beginning. But this is for the best.

Quincy: I'm glad you can see it, but I don't see any future without Daphne in it.

I knew we had plans to meet at the Pond tonight and had every intention of still going. There is absolutely no way I will leave and not say goodbye to her. This may be the last time we EVER see each other. I at least owe her an explanation face to face. I took my shower and acted like I was going to go to bed early. Daddy was gone for one more overnight job and would be back first thing in the morning. I thank God for that because there is no way I would pull this if he was home.

I climbed out the window and started walking towards the Pond. I don't even care if I get in trouble. Because I'm leaving so what could they do? Keep me from Daphne? They're kind of already doing that, so anything else they would do as far as punishment is nothing compared to that.

I was still four of five streets over and already late. I hope she won't leave and think I stood her up. I decided I was going to have to jog to make it in time. Of course, that goes completely against everything I've been taught. Never run because it looks like you just did something. I hadn't been running any time when Aiden and a couple of my teammates pulled up beside me and asked where I was headed. I told them I was headed to one of my friend's house, over by the Pond. He told me to get in, and he would drop me off. I know Daphne never really liked Aiden, and I've never really had a lot of dealings with him, but he seems pretty cool tonight. Maybe he just feels more comfortable having me in his ride being on this side of the tracks, especially at this time of the night. I have no idea what they're doing on this side, but I'm just thanking God and going to call it a blessing; I can make it to Daphne in time and still get back home before Momma even knows I Left.

Meet Me at The Pond

At School, Quincy had really started acting distant the last Month or so. True, we were always careful there, but he was noticeably more distant. He passed me a note in lunch that read, "Meet me at the Pond." We wrote each other notes a lot over the last few years but had a pact that we would tear each one up after reading them. This time, though, I noticed he signed it Quincy. Yes, that's his name, but every other letter until now, he's always signed, "QT" and I can't help but wonder why.

That signature bothered me so much, that I realized I forgot to tear the note up when I threw it away. Surely nobody saw him given it to me. But if they are that desperate to dig through the trash to read the note, they still won't know when we were talking about or why, so it really doesn't matter. I can't help but wonder what's changed. Has he started spending time with Toya? Maybe her persistence finally paid off. Then again, I feel like he knows something. I haven't told anybody. Maybe he can sense something?? My stomach was upset all day. The secret was taking a toll on me, and all this wondering is making me realize I have to tell him. Regardless of the outcome, I have to tell him tonight what happened. I went to the Pond as he asked. The whole walk there, my mind was running. What does he know? What has been bothering him over the last month or so? And last but not least, regardless of what he has to tell me, I have to tell him what happened.

    I stayed for over an hour, and he never showed up. I think back to the last time I saw him. Like I said he was very

distant. I wonder if he wanted to break up with me but just didn't have the nerve to do it face to face. I know he would never stand me up because he's always been so protective of me being out at night alone. Especially on this side of the tracks. The beautiful spot we spent so much time is now as scary and empty as I am.

    To make matters worse, I'm a million percent in love with him, but, sadly, I'm pregnant with Aiden's baby. Me,

pregnant; this is not how I had planned my life. The pregnancy I wish was ours. The only thing that now stands between them, "The US we planned."

Missing love

I hid my pregnancy for as long as I could. I hid my morning sickness and weight gain until I couldn't hide it anymore. I just couldn't bring myself to tell Momma and Daddy. I knew one of the first things they would want to know was by who? They approached me two weeks ago about Quincy. Said one of the workers at the farm told Daddy I was messing around with a black boy. I tried to lie, but I guess it was all over my face because they both tore into me. Said I was a disgrace and embarrassment to the family and dared me to see Quincy again. As much as I hate to admit it, I feel like they will get their wish because I haven't saw Quincy in Month's. It's almost like he fell off the face of the Earth.

They then went on to say Daddy would lose his job if I kept messing around with him. For some reason, Daddy

saying those things didn't surprise me. But to hear Momma talk to me like that, I couldn't believe it. I always thought we had a special connection, but this bit of news has obviously flipped the switch on that.

Finally, I ran away. Not far, just to my best friend Christy's house, a couple of blocks over. When I got there, we sat in her room and just stared at each other. Felt like hours, but I'm sure it was only a few minutes. We decided it would be best if she could break the news to Momma and Daddy. Even though I had practiced saying those two words, "I'm pregnant," repeatedly for the last several months, the only person I told was Christy and I cried to her many times about the situation. She empathized with me but kept telling me how they needed to know. I knew they did but that didn't make it any easier for me to say it. Then, my situation was complicated. I had suffered from a Seizure disorder since I was a kid. They finally got me on the right dosage of medicine a couple years ago and I haven't had one since. I read something about how you can't take certain medicines when your pregnant because it can be dangerous to the baby. Since I hadn't been to the Dr. I just went ahead and kept taking my medicine. I figured it would have to be better than not taking them, having a seizure and falling on my stomach. I'm only 16, and it's so much I don't know, but I'd know; I need to see a Dr. asap.

Christy called and told her I had run away but was with her. She said I was scared because I was pregnant and was

too scared to tell her. When she first called, she put Momma on speakerphone. I couldn't stand to hear her response, so I covered my ears. Even though my ears were covered I, figured I should still be able to hear muffled voices or screams, but I didn't hear a thing. I tried to read Christy's face to guess what Momma said, but there was no reaction. I removed one of my hands from over my ears, and to my surprise, an awkward silence…She said nothing. Just before Christy could say anything else, the phone hung up.

I just knew they would be on their way to get me and was shaking like a leaf. Even though I was relieved, Christy had told her, just knowing they knew and where I was, gave me a whole new level of anxiety. I figured they would come to get me and grill me on how stupid I was, I would never amount to anything, etc. But my anxiety was short-lived because, to my surprise, they never came. I stayed there for two weeks without hearing a peep from them. I wondered was I even welcome home.

Christy's Momma told me she didn't mind me staying at all, but she felt it was only right for me to go home. She

said if I were her daughter, she would want me to be home. Plus, she could get in trouble for having me at her house this whole time. She said she would take me home and speak with Momma before I go in. I didn't want her to get in trouble either, plus, if they didn't want me home, I would know before I even tried to go in since she agreed to talk to Momma first.

To my surprise, Momma said she was fine with me coming home. She said she was disappointed that I was pregnant but said, "What's done was done." Christy and her Momma drove me home, and After some coercing from them, I reluctantly got out of the car and slowly walked with my little brown bag towards the door.

I walked in that day somewhat relieved, but the minute I crossed the doorway, the look of disgust Momma gave me

wasn't enough; the constant put-downs and bickering started. So much so that when I came home from School I, would go in my room and not come out until I knew everyone was asleep. I would walk through the house in the dark and scrounge through the fridge to avoid the looks and put-downs. Or even worse, the painful silence that felt like a dagger in my heart. All this because they think I'm pregnant by Quincy. The love of my life, who has not done anything wrong but be born a different color than me.

All the while, this baby is the product of a rape by someone who looks like me. A rape, I have yet been able to tell

anybody about. I even let Christy think it was by Quincy. How could I not? A rape, I blame myself plenty days for not making sure the basement door was locked. But would it make a difference if they knew? It sickens me to know, if they knew it wasn't by Quincy, they would probably be relieved, and accept the rape over Quincy.

Momma or Daddy never asked me how I felt, if they could feel the baby move, or if the baby ever moved. They

never took me to the Dr, so the baby moving was the only way I knew it was okay. The only thing I knew was the minute I had the baby; I was to come home without it or else. Or else I can't stay there. That was the only conversation we had concerning the pregnancy. It saddens me to no end; I can take them turning their back on me, but to turn their back on what was to be their first Grandchild, is a whole other type of hurt.

Fluffy Cotton and Waterfalls

It's early December, but the School's been out for the last week. We usually start to break Closer to Christmas, but it's been freezing rain and on lately, and the roads are still pretty messed up. Then it's supposed to freeze and snow, so they went ahead and started our break since the buses wouldn't be able to pick everybody up safely. Even though I'm so thankful that I don't have to continue to see all the looks at School, hear all the snide comments, or see Aiden staring at me and my stomach, being home is almost as bad.

The one plus to being home is I can stay in my room and think. I had to eat and bathe, but for the most part, I tried to schedule that around the times when nobody was really around or at work. I don't even know the due date for this pregnancy. Still, a couple of months into the pregnancy, I talked to Mrs. Timms, the School counselor, and she told me she thought I would have the baby at the end of December. She said she had a friend who worked at a health department and had a way to know by when I had my cycle last. She called me to her office a couple more times after that to check on me. She asked me if I was depressed and my plan for when the baby was born. I lied and told her no, I wasn't depressed, and I had everything figured out for the delivery. She did ask me if the father was involved a couple of times, and I lied again. Yes, ma'am, he and his family are very excited". He just lives an hour away, but he comes down to see me most weekends. I feel like she bought it, but my biggest fear is she will reach out to Momma, and she will put a monkey wrench in the whole thing.

It was the first snow of the year, and it was so pretty and fluffy. As far as the eye can see, the ground Looks like it's covered with a blanket of cotton. Our little town was pretty much shut down. The only imperfections in the snow were from where the kids from across the street had been out playing in the front yard earlier.

I put on my big brown boots, coat, earmuffs and step out on the porch. It looks so clean. I take a cleansing breath of the air, and I feel like it made me have icicles in my nose. I do it a couple more times, and I think a

"pop" followed by something warm streaming down my legs. I try to stop it, but I can't. I walk towards the door, and I feel like it's making it worse when I move. I know I'm not peeing on myself because I just used the bathroom before I went outside. On top of that, I could always stop my pee when I needed to, and this won't stop no matter what I do. Plus, I've never used it his much at one time, ever.

I walk towards the door, and my boots are soaking wet and make a sloshy sound each time I step. By the time I cross the doorway into the kitchen, another huge gush starts. Momma was washing the dishes, but when that water started running again, she just stopped. She held her head back, put the dish-towel down, and held onto the counter. I was frozen stiff. She slowly turned around and looked at the floor, then me. She told me. Well, Miss lady, your world is definitely about to change. She threw me a towel and told me to clean up the floor then, get another towel and put it between my legs. I shuffle to the bathroom and wash up. I realized it was getting close to time to have

the baby because I heard Momma talking to Aunt Betty on the phone and asking Uncle Paul to take me to the Hospital. I ran back to my room and looked at the book Momma Timms gave me. Toward the back, it talked about the baby being in the water, and before the baby is born, the bag has to break open. I start to wonder, is this really about to happen?? Today?? I'm not hurting, though. I've always heard it hurts awful bad to have a baby, so this must not be it. I tiptoe back towards the kitchen, and I can see Momma sitting at the table with her head down. I accidentally startled her. She looks up at me, and her eyes go straight to my stomach. She stands back up, turns her back to me, and starts back watching dishes. As I turn to walk away, she tells me to pack a bag to go to the Hospital because my ride will be here soon. I go to the room and pick up my old book bag, but I have no idea what I'm supposed to be packing.

Earline RN...Nurse to Nurse report

Earline: I take pride in my job. At times I feel I have a hard time cutting loose at the end of the shift because I have a mental checklist of things' I've always prided myself in completing before I leave. Sadly though, many times, it's still never enough. Somebody always finds something I didn't do or should have done differently. Not to mention not being able to find something they thought I didn't chart. I know I'm not perfect, I do make mistakes, but I did chart it most of the time, just not in a spot they would have.

RN, I wear these letters with pride. I worked very hard to get them letters true enough, but I can't forget those who suffered a great deal to pave the way for this to even be possible. On my most challenging workday, I am very aware; this is a true calling for me. Having the most rewarding career, so many before me could only dream about. Many of which may have performed so many of the same tasks I do daily. Self-taught, determined, empathetic. Yet, not ever recognized for their services.

Earline, you got yourself a real winner!! I've taken care of her for 12 hours, and she hasn't said two words to me. Daphne: The door opened, and before I opened my eyes, I lay there and pretended it would be Quincy. I squeezed them shut. I heard footsteps getting closer to the bed, so I figured I better open my eyes. It was a nurse. A short, plump, brown lady with long wavy hair. Had they sent her in here because they heard about me and Quincy?

I'm relieved. The other lady I had, I felt like she looked down her nose at me all day. She never even tried to talk to me. Just barked at me. Of course, I know I wasn't very talkative, but I wanted to be. She didn't even try to figure me out. What 16year-old wants to be here by herself having a baby? But his lady I think I can open up to. Her eyes tell me I can trust her, and not only is she walking towards me, but she's smiling at me. She makes it to the bed and lays her hand on mine. It's almost like she's pumping energy and purpose into me with her touch. I exhale and sit up in bed.

Earline: Hi, my name is Earline, I'm going to be your nurse and take care of you tonight. How are you feeling?

Daphne: I'm okay but so tired

Earline: Yea, I heard you've had a long day but were going to see what we can do to make you as comfortable as possible. Is there anything I can do for you right now?

Daphne: Yes, can you please do something to speed this up? Earline: laughing. No sweetie. That's not up to me. That's up to your body and the little one.

Daphne: (looking down with disgust)

Earline: But I tell you what, one thing I can do is make sure I'm here for whatever you need until that happens. Is that okay with you?

Daphne: Yes, ma'am, it is. Thank you.

Go Time

This pain is terrible!! I feel like I'm being punished for something I had no control over. Each time I have those pains, I feel like I'm going to die. Just when the pain stops, all I can do is catch my breath, and like a thief in the night, it comes again. I look at the old dusty clock in the corner, and the numbers are so dim. I feel like me and the clock are on our last leg. Rightfully so since it says 3:52 am, which means I've been here for over 16 hours and still no baby. I honestly don't think I can take much more. I'm to the point where I want just to ask them to cut this thing out of me!! I don't even want to look at it because the creation of it changed my life as I once knew it. What type of person am I to think like that??

I wish I had my Momma here. It's crazy for me even to think that we used to be so close given the last few months, but, believe it or not before this, I never had to turn to anybody for help or advice because she was my go-to. Sadly though, ever since she got a whiff of me and Quincy, all that changed. In the beginning, it was just the side looks and racist remarks. As time went on and she realized I was pregnant, she couldn't even look at me without disgust. I guess, in my mind, I thought things would change when it was closer to time. Even with all the months of us not having the same relationship we had, I still need her. I know I let her down by being young and pregnant. I know I did because I let myself down too, but how can a baby, regardless of how it was made, be such a horrible thing?

  Maybe she doesn't have the same love for me I still have for her. Ever since I was a little girl, I've thought about this

moment. I always imagined Momma and my husband would be by my side when I had my precious baby. That's all I've ever wanted to do was be a Momma. I always thought this would be one of the happiest days of my life. Never in my wildest dreams did I think I would be 16, alone, and feeling this worthless and empty.

  I look up, and Earline is walking in. She looks at me, and I feel like she can read my mind. She quickly comes over

to the bed and looked me in the eyes. She asked me if she could do an exam because she thinks we may be close. I nod yes. She goes to the closet, places on her glove and quickly turns around towards me with a sense of purpose. Her hand enters me, but this time her eyes don't look the same as the others before her, and it didn't take as long. She removes her glove, looks at me, and says. "I know you've had a rough time, but baby, you're at the end now." She gets a cold towel and wipes sweat from my brow. She then wraps the towel around my neck. Oh my God, that towel gave me my second wind. I know it sounds crazy, but I feel like it's helping me in some way. How could something like a wet towel even help something like this? She yells down the hall for the delivery room to be set up and for them to give the Dr an update.

  I'm starting to feel panic, but when I look at her, I feel I will be okay. She looks at me like she would take the pain

away if she could, and I believe she would. Other than Christy, this is the only time I've felt that someone cared about how I have felt over the last nine months. But I even had guilt about Christy being by my side. I felt horrible knowing the baby was by Aiden. They didn't last long after that night. She later told me he tried to take things too far, but she wasn't ready then. She said the next few weeks, he acted like everything was okay, but she later heard he had been with a girl from the next town over. She did still love him, though, and I wanted so bad to be able to take her pain away by telling her how much of an ASS he was, but I also couldn't break her heart by letting her know I kept this from her this whole time. I just kept letting her think the baby was by Quincy. Plus, that way, she would understand somewhat why I couldn't keep the baby.

Earline: Aside: look at her. Frail, pale, looks unkempt, and nobody's here with her. What's her story? I'm a black nurse who's been taking care of her for the last 8 hours, and she's been extremely friendly to me, given the circumstances. Hasn't even flinched when I've touched her, which is unlike most before her. She even allowed me to help her in the bath earlier. Why is she okay with me taking care of her?

I never had a daughter and may not know what to even do with one, but I could take her home, in all honesty, fatten her up a bit. More importantly, build her up. She's obviously been beaten down to the max!! She's here, but not here at the same time. She looks like a lost child. I can't explain it. Her eyes are so distant, mysterious, and empty, but way full too. They have a story to tell. I don't know it, but it sure looks dark. My biggest question of the day is, where this girl's Momma

is??

Okay, Daphne honey, I know you've been through the wringer with this pain, and I know you feel like throwing in the towel, but this is GO TIME. I need you to dig deep. You're the only person that has the best ability to get this baby out. I need you to do as I tell you. It's going to be hard, but you can do this. I'm not leaving your side, and we're going to do this together, okay. I have faith in you; now place your trust in God. He will get you through this.

Daphne: I thought I knew how she would change things for me earlier, but with those words for once in this whole 9-month process, she gave me the gift for me to believe in me. Just then, I felt my body start to shake. I tried to stop it but couldn't. I kind of feel like I may be getting ready to have a Seizure! I sure hope not because I haven't had one in years, and I haven't missed a dose of my medicine. Then, to top it all off, I feel like I need to have a bowel movement. Do I need to tell her so I can go to the bathroom? Now the pain is coming back-to-back, and I'm starting to feel like I'm about to pass out!! I'm starting to grunt and bear down and not even trying!!

Mommmmaaaa, I scream, but why because she isn't there...Please God help me!! I push for hours. A few times I

pushed so hard that I felt like my head was going to explode. Then I keep getting told I'm almost there. I like Earline but I'm starting to think she's not telling me the whole truth. I don't think this baby is ever going to come out.

Earline: When I was beginning to feel it was hopeless, she starts to grunt differently, and I can tell in her face that she has her second wind. I reach down to check her, and the pad underneath her is soaked with warm, clear fluid and blood. With this exam, I can reach the baby's head without difficulty, and there is now a great deal of pressure behind it. Completely opposite of all her previous exams. The baby has descended way down in her pelvis. With one extra practice push, I feel more pressure. I pull the sheet back, and with her last effort, I can now see tons of dark hair.

I yell down the hall to call the Dr. ASAP. Lord, I hope he's close and not in a bad mood. I honestly don't think I can stand here and listen without a response tonight. I've been Earline RN (Real nice) every shift for the last several years, but today I might turn into THE EARLINE-no filter; let me tell you all about yourself from back in the day. Even though I've always followed the rules, I keep a little of that "Get back," in my right pinky toe. Lord knows I can pull it out when I need to, and I think tonight would qualify for one of those times!! They said Dr. Hunter was on the floor and headed to the delivery room. This being her first baby and so young, I doubt she would deliver before he got in the room, but I didn't want to take any chances.

I can tell by her reaction that the pressures worse, but she's still able to breathe through the contractions. I'm able to

clean her bottom, change her pad and drain her bladder while Dr. Hunter is putting on his gown. I place her in stirrups and stand between her legs attentively until he's dressed. Once he is, I gladly allowed him to take my place. I hurriedly secure the nape of his gown and hand him his gloves. I think I can speak for every Nurse when I say, no matter how prepared you think you are for delivery, when the Dr. makes it to the room, you still feel somewhat unprepared. I know I get a whole little nervous flutter in my spirit when they walk in. It's the absolute fear of them needing something they never, ever need but do at that time, and it, whatever that may be, is not available in the room.

As I take my place at her side, he glanced over at me, and I can tell the way his left brow raises, what he's thinking. He's never been one to mask or hide how he feels in the delivery room. He's sure she's not ready because the head is not visible. He hates when he's called to a room too early. Just then, she starts to grunt, and her legs go stiff as aboard. Her ordinarily pale and emotionless face is now beat red, mouth pursed tight, and with tears streaming down her face and clear liquid coming out of her left nostril. She is, pushing with all she had in her, and at that moment, the head and ears were visible. He attempts to redirect her to relax her bottom, breathe, and push. I honestly don't think she was listening to anything he said. She was ultimately out of control. She looked at me as if to say, help me. I obtained the nitrous and asked if she had changed her mind. She shook her head rapidly. I placed the mask on her and had her take three deep cleansing breaths. She started to relax and was able to listen to his directions a little better.

Daphne: I should have tried the gas earlier. It takes some of the pain away and helps me to relax a little bit. Either way, gas or not, I don't like the Dr. He is not very friendly. He doesn't say anything, just sits and looks at me; I think I'm getting on his nerves because I keep raising my bottom off the bed when he puts his hand inside me. He acts like I'm some low-class piece of trash that he could care less about. I'm starting to feel like my bottom is on fire. They tell me to keep pushing, but I don't like that feeling, so I try not to, but my body won't let me stop. I feel like I'm about to pass out and can't catch my breath when they do tell me to stop. I feel the worst pressure that I ever had, and Earline looks at me with pity.

Earline: Even though she was giving it her all, the baby was now not budging. At this point, I think I was pushing and sweating harder than she was because I knew what was coming next. I knew I didn't call him too early, but I wanted to coach her into getting the baby out. Pussshhhh honey!! The baby is almost here. Don't give up now. I know you're tired, but it's almost over! You can do this!! You're stronger than you think you are! Listen to your body and do what it tells you to do.

I always hated this part, but it had to be done. He looks at me and extends an open hand. I hand him the scissors

without her seeing them. He places them between her leg; they made gut-cringing gristle like cutting noise that you can never be prepared for no matter how many times you hear it—followed by the clinking together of scissors tossed in a metal pan and piercing scream that always cut right through my soul.

Doctor Hunter's gruff, muffled voice said. "Had to be done, no way around it." Even though I haven't liked his bedside manner in the past, this time, without a doubt, he was 1000 percent right because, with the next push, the baby's head descends, and with two more contractions, a new miracle entered the world. Naturally, this is when the Dr, announces what the sex of the baby is, but the baby came out almost lifeless so that was the least of his worries.

Daphne: I look over at the Dr, and he seems like he's struggling. Then they tell me to lay down, but that scares me.

I want to be able to see what's going on. Another nurse comes in, looks at the clock and yells something. Then her and Earline lay me back in a hurry. All the while, the Dr. is yelling at them to give him some pressure. The other Nurse jumps on top of me and pushes down on the bottom of my belly so hard that I can see the frown lines on her forehead and sweat on her top lip. I have no idea what's happening, but I feel like something is wrong.

They then start to push my legs back with so much force they were almost to my shoulders. Now I can see the Dr,

and he too looks worried and has sweat dripping from his forehead. He grabbed my right hand and placed it between my legs. I felt something cold, round, and wet. He said, your baby is stuck, and I have to get it out now!!! What did he mean stuck??? How long has the head been there? Can the baby breathe? Is it going to come out??

Please, Lord, help me through this!! I feel like me and the baby are both about to die. I feel the sharp scissors cutting

me then they yell for me to push some more. I'm crying so bad and not sure I can. Earline pulls me to her and says," Listen to me. You are the only one that can do this!! You've made it through this pregnancy and will make it through this delivery. You can do it now make it happen for your baby!! She placed that same wet towel around my neck, and again with her words, I found some newfound strength.

I took a huge deep breath and pushed as hard as I ever thought I would!! There was a huge relief and a large gush of

warm water. It's out. Omg I can't believe it. All that pressure and pain ended 10 seconds ago and I feel relieved already. I had my eyes closed but opened them when I felt the baby be born. I looked straight up at the ceiling, tears streaming down my face without me even trying. I hear some scuffling and moving about but still no baby noises. They weren't that far from me, but I still couldn't look. My eyes wanted me to, but my mind wouldn't let me. I couldn't keep my mind from wondering if the baby was even alive. Maybe I was being punished, because how I felt the whole pregnancy. Maybe God is going to just take it away, so I won't have to regret my decision to leave the baby here.

I decided to glace up, and saw Earline rush over to grab the baby and took it to the baby bed looking thing with the

light on it. I couldn't see much, but I could see her rubbing the baby with blankets, throwing the blankets down, and grabbing others. She rubbed on the baby real hard and fast and looked like she was talking to the baby, but I couldn't hear what she was saying.

    I start to wonder if then Momma and Daddy will look at me again. If the baby's not there, then maybe I won't be

such a disappointment to them. Maybe things can be back like they were before they found out about me and Quincy. I picture me and Momma sitting at the kitchen table looking through the ads and cutting out coupons. Making a shopping list and watching our favorite tv shows. We didn't have money, but we were so close. She was my best friend until she found out about us. Just then I'm jolted back to reality when I hear the baby start to cry. A small whimper. Then a louder cry. I could see the look of pure joy and relief on Earline's face, so I laid back in bed and cried like a baby!!

Earline: I don't care how good of a Dr. or Nurse you are; you get scared when you get a terrible baby. He rubs the baby's back. Gentle at first and then more vigorous. Still nothing. I can see it's a girl. I reached for her then carried her in a hurry to the warmer and continued to dry and stimulate her. She started to whimper, then cry, and few more seconds she was letting her presence be known by using those healthy lungs. In no time she was starting to really pink up. I felt like she was stable so I took her over to mom in an attempt to place her on her chest. She shook her head vigorously, almost crawled up the bed, and turned away from me. Almost like she's seen a ghost!! Maybe with her being so young, she wants her cleaned up first. I take her over to the warmer so I can look her over under better lighting. There is no one here to trim the excess cord, so I do it. I run some warm water in a tiny bowl and begin to bathe her and wash her hair. She's so content after her bath. I say a small prayer for her as I did all my babies; I took care of every day that I worked.

"Lord, this is your child. I know you have a plan that will allow him or her to grow up and do great things for you. Lord, I thank you for blessing this family with him or her and thank you for allowing me to be a part of witnessing your miracle with each delivery".

Amen.

> She looks like a doll!! Look at her!! Ivory skin, dark hair, chubby cheeks, full lips w one dimple, and beautiful big

hazel brown eyes. No blemishes or newborn rash. The only thing I find is a small birthmark under her left breast and a more noticeable birthmark on her right wrist, in the shape of a perfectly shaped heart. It even had a reddish, purple hue that's unbelievable to witness. I almost couldn't take my eyes off of it. How neat is it to have a heart-shaped birthmark?? I turn her over to evaluate her back, and there sat a large, blue/green area on the top of her backside: a classic, Mongolian spot. Nowwwww things are making a little more sense. No wonder she has been fine with me caring for her. I look further, and her ears and genitalia have a faint tint I'm familiar with. I haven't seen it much in these times, but I know it when I see it. I swaddle her and hand her to her Momma. This time she shakily accepts her. She holds her close but never looks down at her. She continues to look straight ahead, and those tears start to come on their own without her even trying. I don't think she got enough energy to even change her facial expression.

She's so young I'm sure she's terrified. Especially not having any support here with her. I sit for a bit to make sure

she's okay with her. She was already pale before she delivered and looks even more so now, but her bleeding is okay. I'm beginning to think she's just in disbelief from the full delivery and wiped out.

I started to walk out, but then I reach over as a gesture to see if she wants me to take her back. She hands her to me very quickly. I look down at the baby, and she's content. I lay her in the Bassinet next to her mother's bed. I have about 30 min before I have to recheck her blood pressure, so that gives me just enough time to relive this bladder, massage this left foot and eat a bite or two of my cheese and crackers.

Never Look Back

They offered to wheel me downstairs, but I declined. I didn't want to play out any of the, "I just had a baby movie." Of course, I did but I didn't want anyone to ask me about the baby, how I felt or if the baby was sick and needed to stay in the hospital etc. I needed to walk away and never look back for my own sanity...

Things got worse after I walked out those doors. I sat for hours waiting on a ride...Never came. I decided to walk

home. At the time, it seemed like a good idea. A Lot better than waiting for a ride that may never come. The walk home was probably a little over a mile, but it felt like a lot longer. The wind cut my cheeks like a knife, and my fingers were so numb they felt like they would snap in two. With each cleansing breath I took, it felt like ice crystals were forming in my nose hairs. Each step took me farther from her and closer to the small green house, at the end of the winding road, that I use to consider home.

Even though the house hadn't had very good memories over the last nine months, I was still relieved when I started

to see a glimpse of the smoke coming from the chimney. Partly because I felt weak, and lightheaded. I realized I hadn't ate or drank anything since yesterday. Then to make matters worse, my pad was completely soaked with blood.

Part II

Vanessa's Breath of Fresh Air

Every now and then, I go for a walk around the neighborhood to get a little fresh air and a little exercise. We live in a pretty nice size city, but our community is kind of like a small city all its own. Always been proud to say I was born and raised in Brunsonville Heights. Where everybody knows everybody on a first-name basis, and everybody looks out for one another. Everything we need is pretty much within a couple of blocks. The Hospital, School, and light company are all around the corner, the grocery store is a little further down the street, and the corner store is at the end of our block. Never really had a name; we all just called it the corner store for as long as I can remember. The owners are a cute little white, elderly couple, and they are really sweet. They know us all by name, know our family, and we all have a tab there. Any extra money kids get, they always headed there to buy penny candy, pickles, juice, or single cookies out of the tall, clear cookie containers with the red top and silver handle.

I've walked this stretch three times today and decided to call it a day. I turn the corner to head back home, and I see Momma Gladys. It was always a pleasure to chat with her. I've known her my whole life. Her and my Momma were always good friends, and that says a lot. Don't get me wrong, Momma is sweet, but she don't trust too many people and sticks close to home. But Momma Gladys, she can't get enough of. Always on the phone, sharing recipes, what stores got the best deals this week, followed by how they think the Reverend did with Sunday service. She was kind of like the neighborhood Grandmother, in a way. She had two kids of her own that were grown now. But somehow, she had become the lady that all the little girls brought their babies to. Everybody called her Momma Gladys as well as me. She was in her early to mid-'70s and walked w a slight limp. I can't remember a time; I didn't see her in anything other than a dress with a worn apron and a tight headwrap. Along the edges, you could see coarse, tight salt and pepper curls. Her skin was smooth, not a wrinkle to be found, and walnut color. She had powerful features but a pleasant spirit about herself. Most days, she sat on her stoop in the front yard fanning with at least 3-4 kids sitting close to her or running around playing.

Today she was hanging clothes on the line. She had a large basket beside her full to the rim and looked as if she was struggling. So, I walked over to ask if she needed help. She said she was fine, but I noticed a deep thought type crease above her left brow, so I went ahead and started helping her. I noticed most of the clothes were baby clothes—tiny baby clothes at that.

I didn't know she had any small babies. As a matter of fact, I hadn't known any of the neighborhood kids to be expecting lately. She told me some ladies from Social Services had heard about her and came by to ask her to help them with their foster program. She said she was getting ready to have a baby girl next week. She talked with excitement but seemed anxious all the same. She went on to tell me that she loves kids and doesn't mind helping, but she likes to do things on her terms and didn't want to have all kinds of folks in and out of her house snooping around. She said it wasn't many people wanting older kids, but everybody wants a baby, so she figured the baby may not stay long that's one of the reasons she decided to go ahead and take the baby in.

Momma Gladys: Chile, you ought to get you a baby.

Vanessa: Momma Gladys, you know I can't have any babies. Remember, I had those tumors and had to have surgery years ago.

Momma Gladys: I know that honey. I'm talking about some of these babies these folks got. It's a lot of these kids, they say. I can't take no more than one at a time since they are so little. Mixed breeds and folks don't want them. Say it's a lot of problems being all mixed up like that. The black folks ok with them but the white folks shole don't want em.

Vanessa: I would be ok with the baby no matter what the race was, but it's all the in and out the house I wouldn't like.

Momma Gladys: This one I'm getting ain't but two weeks old.

Vanessa: Two weeks old? Wow... I wonder why is she being placed somewhere?

Momma Gladys: Honey, I don't even ask no more. It's so much that goes on. I used to ask years ago, but it made me so sad I wanted to keep all of them, and I knew I couldn't, so I just stopped asking.

Vanessa: I finish helping her hang the clothes and head over to the corner store to grab a few items. The whole time I kept thinking about what Momma Gladys said, "You should get you one of those babies." Lord knows, I always wanted a baby. Me and Richard started trying as soon as we got married. Still, shortly after that, I started having issues and had to have a female surgery and lost all my parts. I was tore up and depressed about it for a while. In the beginning, I wouldn't eat or get out of bed. I lost so much weight but had no idea how small I was. One day I got on the scale, and it said 95 pounds!! My nerves were absolutely shot, and it wasn't long before I had to be put on nerve pills. Richard was a good, hardworking man who came from a close family. My biggest fear was that he would leave me since I couldn't give him a baby. He always told me that would never happen, but it was still always in the back of my mind.

> Momma was a foster parent too. That's how her and Momma Gladys got so close. She got several kids in and out

over the years, and I helped her a lot. Momma said she wouldn't have been able to do it all if it hadn't been for me helping with the kids. She felt the best thing for me and Richard was to adopt. She knew how bad we wanted kids and about me not being able to have any after the surgery.

At first, I didn't even mention it to him. I guess I was starting to consider it and didn't want him to shut down the idea before being mentally ready to accept a no. Momma usually got older kids. Teenage kids that stayed a while. So long that, most time, they aged out of the system, or somebody in the family, finally took them in. Then, one time, she got smaller kids. Two and Three- year old siblings. A boy and girl named: Byron and Samantha. I found myself getting attached to them. And he did too. A month or so after they came, I decided to mention it to Richard, after-all. At first, he was entirely against it. He said you never know what you're getting with foster kids and didn't want to have issues with their family coming to get them etc. Well, I knew the kid's situation, and I knew there was no chance the family could get them back. Plus, they were from out of state, so there would be no way to find them here. Then Momma said there was a way that the records could be sealed, so even if they did decide to look for them when they got older, there would be no way.

We talked about it a few other times over the next couple of months, and finally, he decided we could start the

process. I was surprised that it didn't take long, and, in a couple, short months, all the paperwork was done, and we were officially parents. A boy and a girl are all I ever wanted. Richard came from a larger family than me and always said he didn't want any more than one or two, so this was perfect.

A few years went by, and all was well. Until I saw Momma Gladys that day. Once we talked and she mentioned a

baby to me, my mind started running overtime. I came home that day, and it was all I could think about. I was too scared to mention it to Richard. So, I talked to Momma about it. She was happy and said she thought we should look into it and that she would help as much as she could. Said she would keep the baby, so we could still work but wouldn't have to pay for child-care.

I stewed over it for a week or so, and while on my Sunday stroll, I decided I would go see Momma Gladys. I've

mentally made all these plans about a baby she mentioned she thought she was getting. But heck, I don't even know if she actually even got the baby since we last talked. I knocked on the door and was told to come in. I opened the door, and the smell of burning wood filled the room. A faint glow from the wood-burning fireplace allowed me to see Momma Gladys Silhouette in her rocker, rocking a baby. My heart started to race, and I couldn't get to her fast enough. She was happy to see me, she said. I never even looked at her. My eyes focused right in on the baby.

There she was. The baby I've been thinking about for weeks but never met. The one I'd envisioned myself rocking

all my life. Momma Gladys immediately handed her to me. She said she came two days ago, and she's been meaning to call me but was so tied up between the baby and the other toddlers she had recently got. She said her name was Jennifer, and she was two weeks old. She was in a Jade sleeper, which Ironically happens to be my favorite color. Of course, I felt like that was a sign since that color is so rare. She's so tiny. Her skin was like peaches and cream, pale but still somewhat pink.

Momma Gladys said she had just finished feeding her, and she had a good appetite. I'm sure how she could tell I was staring at the baby like I was a kid in a candy store. I felt like I could hold her all day. She then crept up from the rocker and offered me her seat. I declined, but she wouldn't have it. She said she was glad I stopped because she needed to use the restroom and was hating to put her down since the other kids were running around. I went ahead and took her up on her offer.

I held her close to me and started to rock her. She smelled like Ivory soap and baby powder. Her hair was sandy and felt like silk. There wasn't much of it, but she had the cutest little curl at the top. Her belly was tight, but she was sleeping so soundly. She started to move her head from side to side but snuggled into my chest and remained asleep. I held her extra close, covered her with the receiving blanket, and closed my eyes.

Dear God,

Thank you for all you have done for me and my family. Thank you for clothing and keeping me in my right mind. Thank you for blessing me with a wonderful Husband and two amazing kids and for those reasons I am forever grateful. I also come before you today with a need and ask that you allow this need to be met in your name. Please, God, I ask for you to intervene in this situation to enable me to have a hand in this baby's life. We need her, and I know she needs us. There is no way we would ever let anything happen to her. I will ALWAYS do everything in my power to protect her. I don't know her circumstances before now, but our whole goal will be to make sure she never lacks love or support from now on. This I ask in Jesus's name.

Amen

I open my eyes and looked back down, baby Jennifer. Somewhere between the beginning of my prayer and now, her beautiful, full, bright hazel brown eyes are fixed right on me. Almost as if she is saying she's holding me to those promises I just made with God. My heart melted, and at that very moment, I immediately fell in love. There was no turning back on my end, and even though I knew it would be a task to win Richard over on this one, I had faith, he and the kids would love her just as much as I did. Momma Gladys had obviously been standing in the doorway, watching me with her for a bit. She put her hand on my shoulder and told me she knew this baby was meant for me. Confirmation for me, if I ever needed it. Just knowing Momma Gladys knew I could do this was what I needed at that moment. She told me she would talk to the social worker in the morning and tell her she had a couple interested in the baby. She didn't think she would keep her much longer with the other toddlers in the home. She also said she would have the social worker call me tomorrow to meet and go over the details.

I laid her down in her Bassinet and just watched her for a couple more minutes. Momma Gladys said she thought this baby would have a blessed life. She picked her up and turned her towards me. I hope she's not trying to give her to me again because if so, I would gladly take her and never make it home. She asked me to turn on the small oil lamp sitting in the corner. When I turned back around, she was in the process of taking the Jade sleeper off. As I said before, she was such a chunky little thing. She backed for me to come closer, faced her bare arm towards me. At first, I thought I had to be seeing things. I know I've been thinking about this baby a lot, and she already has a place in my heart, but I literally see what looks to be a heart on her wrist. How could that be possible? Momma Gladys said she felt it was a mark that meant the baby was genuinely made out of love but born to fill the empty place in my heart.

Momma Gladys- She's your child, baby I just know she is. All you have to do is name it, claim it, and God will see that she's yours.

I walked out of Momma Gladys' house a completely different person. Even though tears filled my eyes, I had an extra pep in my step. I accepted the words Momma Gladys just gave me and believed in my heart baby Jennifer was meant to be a part of our family. I would finally have my chance to Mother, an infant. Now all I had to do was convince my husband…Before tomorrow.

> I hadn't made it to the next block by the time the Devil started putting doubt in my mind. Who am I fooling? My

health isn't the best. Sure, we work hard and always have, but still, it's hard to make ends meet at times. We never even had a place of our own. It benefited all of us to stay together since we all split the bills. Then with times being hard everywhere, that helped them and us. And I helped them, and they could help us. We all got along fine, but some people may not understand the dynamics. I'm sure the Social Services Investigator will look at all that as a way to tell us NO!! No way they are going to let us have her.

But I want her so BAD!! She's a tiny baby. Something I've always wanted, and in my eyes, she's perfect. I wanted to have a baby of my own, but it wasn't in God's plan. Sometimes I felt like I was being punished for some reason. Everybody around me was able to, and I know, for a fact, some of them didn't deserve a child. I helped raise so many kids and felt like I would do a great job only if given a chance.

Nervous Wreck

Just as she said she would , Momma Gladys called me a little before noon. She said the Social worker actually wanted to meet us today at her house around 5. I immediately agreed. That time couldn't be more perfect. Richard usually gets off at 4:30, but since work was slow, they had got off all week at 3. My nerves were a wreck. I tried to keep myself busy, so I cleaned, did laundry, and did a roller set on my hair. I found Richard a nice pair of slacks and a plaid shirt. I wanted the meeting to be as smooth as possible, so I made sure everything he needed was within arm's reach of where he usually sits after work. I didn't think we would be able to concentrate if we took Byron and Samantha. You can only keep a six- & eight year-old quiet for so long before they get antsy. Or, in their case, start arguing. Momma knew we had the meeting, so she said it was ok for them to stay home with her.

We head over to Momma Gladys'. As soon as we pulled up, she met us at the door with Jennifer. She invited us in and immediately handed her to me, then ran off to the kitchen. She said she was making some dressing and needed to check on it. Her house did smell amazing. I've never had her chicken and dressing, but I know it was going to be good just like everything else she makes. Over the years, at church functions, she always brought the best dishes. Then around the Holiday Season, she even sold full dinners, cakes, pies, butter rolls, and banana pudding. She was always one of the best cooks we all knew. I gave the baby to Richard and he held her the whole meeting. He kept a permanent smile the whole time we were there. Whenever there was a time when we weren't talking, he kept mentioning how cute she was and her fat jaws.

The meeting went really well. The Social Service worker gave us a picture of the baby, and we signed paperwork to start the process. She said she would use that information for our background check. The next step will be to come to our house for a formal visit to meet the kids. She would also tour the place to make sure there weren't any hazard risks. She mentioned she would have her Boss with her, and it would be a good idea for us to have the area we plan to call her space ready for her, clean, free of any clutter, etc.

Richard-Finding the Lost Spark

Vanessa might have a heart attack if they tell us, no, and I won't know what to do then. She's been in a pretty good place, but she has a nerve problem and has been on medicine for it for a while. Then, she has pretty much been sick off and on her whole life. The funny thing is, in all our years of marriage, the only time I saw her eyes light up the way they are now is the day we met and when we got the kids. Over the years, she seemed to have lost that spark in her eye, though. I always went out of my way to bring her gifts and cater to her, but it still felt like something was missing no matter what. Like I couldn't break through and make her light up again.

Today though, when she held Jennifer, there it was again. Just as bright and beautiful as the day we met. Now I feel that spark in me that I've been chasing all these years too. I can't help but wonder if, through all my prayers to fix Vanessa, God answered my prayers to heal us both. I was so worried about fixing and making her happy; in turn, I feel this baby will improve something in me; I didn't even realize was broken. I know we can take care of her well. She won't have to want for anything, and we will always make her feel loved. Now, all we have to do is convince them of that. Since I've got a taste of this feeling, it's addictive, and I don't know what I will do if this opportunity falls through.

A Go or No

The ride home was quiet. I wondered what Richard was thinking. I wasn't sure if he wanted to pull out already or

not. He's always been a man of few words, but this is unlike him. I can't read him at all this time. He acted like he thought she was so precious when he met her. But does being adorable win her entrance into our lives?

We made it home in no time since Momma Gladys doesn't live that far from us. I thought maybe we would ride a few blocks so we could talk before getting home. Richard wasn't saying anything, and it was killing me because I wanted to know what he was thinking so bad. On the other hand, I didn't want to push him into something he didn't want to do or make him feel like I was rushing him into talking when he may be still processing the whole thing.

Once we parked, we both just sat in the car. Richard turned to me and said, "I'm ok with it, but we need to talk to the kids to see what they think first."

Vanessa: Richard, they are kids. They are too young to be the determining factor for something like this.

Richard: I didn't say they would make the entire decision; I'm just saying they should have some input too. All our lives would change with a new baby. They are just starting to be more independent in some areas, but pretty soon they will need us to go to more School functions and stuff and I don't want them to feel like they are being replaced with a baby.

Vanessa: I really don't think they will think that. Samantha absolutely loves babies, and remember how good Byron was with her?

Richard: Yea, you're right. But I will just have to wait until after we talk with them to decide.

Vanessa: Of course, I don't have a problem with that because they need to feel they have a say in the whole thing.

The kids are ok and we haven't had many issues lately. Then again, at this point, I have no idea what they may say. Of course, that scares me to death because Richard is serious about them being involved and getting their approval before moving forward with the foster plan. We called the kids in the living room to talk to them about having the baby stay with us. Vanessa: Ok, kids, me and your Daddy need to talk to you about something. At first, they just stared at me, then each other, then Samantha blurted out, "Whatever it is, I didn't do it."

Byron: Naw, wait a minute, I didn't do anything either. I've been in my room watching T.V. and playing with my cars. Vanessa: Now, did I say yall did something?? We wanted to talk to you about a little baby named Jennifer that me and your

Daddy just met. We are wondering if yall would be ok if she came and stayed with us.

Blank looks from both of them with complete silence. I've prayed for some peace and quiet around this house for years, but this was not what I had in mind. To make things worse, Richard is now not only up, out of his chair, but pacing a hole in the carpet.

Vanessa: Look, the baby doesn't have anywhere to go, and since we have room, I figured we could help Momma Gladys out and let her stay here.

Samantha: Where is her Momma? Why does Momma Gladys get her? Why does she need help if she such a little baby, and how long is she staying with us?

Vanessa: Well, we all know Momma Gladys keeps kids a lot. I'm not sure how she got Jennifer, but the plan was to stay with Momma Gladys until they could find somewhere else to put her. Then it doesn't help that she's older and already had her hands full with those two little boys she brings to the Church.

Samantha and Byron: (in unison)- OOH yea, and they are baddddd…

Vanessa laughs, and Richard has a big smile on his face.

Vanessa: It's nice to see the two of you can agree on something but look whos' talking about somebody being bad-(with a smile.) Well, she didn't know how long she would be able to keep the baby because she's nervous the older kids may accidentally hurt her when she's not watching. Since yall are older than they are, I know she will be safe with yall. As far as how long she may stay with us, I'm not sure but hopefully for a long time.

Richard: We really don't know. It could be a while, or a week or two. It just depends on how long Momma Gladys needs help.

Samantha: Well, I know I will be good with her because I take real good care of my baby dolls.

Vanessa: I wanted to laugh so bad, but she was so serious, so I just smiled.

I looked over at Richard, and he's smiling too. I'm hoping this is breaking the ice. Looks like Samantha is all in. Now we just have to get Byron on board. I can't really read him on this one. I turn to look at him.

Byron: Where is she planning on sleeping? We don't have a baby bed, and I just got my own room, so I don't want to share it already.

Vanessa: Don't worry, Byron, you won't have to share your room. She will stay in our room in her Bassinet. Momma Gladys already has all the things she needs at her place, and anything else she needs, we will buy.

Byron: It's ok with me then. I just didn't want to have to share my room. But before she comes, can yall talk to

Samantha and tell her to stop asking for so much stuff. I know with a new baby here, we are going to have to try and save money, and we can't with her always asking for stuff.

Samantha: Shut up! I don't ever ask for anything. Your just mad because Momma wouldn't buy you that race car toy but bought me a dress for Church.

Byron: It isn't just the race car; you're always getting stuff because you're the girl, and when I want something, we can't afford it, or I got to wait till later.

Richard looks at Vanessa, puts his head in his hands, and shakes his head.

Vanessa: Ok, now, stop it, you two! Take some time and think about somebody else for a change. This baby ain't got nowhere else to go, and all yall can think about is yourselves. We are in a position to help, so we are. I trust yall will be gentle with her and help us take just as good of care as we take of yall.

Richard: We are all going to have to pitch in and help. She is a small baby, so we may be a little more tired than usual since she may have some nights where she may not sleep well. Yall can help by helping with bottles or grabbing a diaper here and there for us.

Samantha: That's Byron because I want to help. I like babies. Especially baby girls. I want to hold her and comb her hair and give her a bath, and…

Vanessa: Well, Samantha, you will eventually help with all that, but right now, we have to start off slow and let her get a little bigger. As small as she is, she could get hurt very easily.

Samantha: Ok, but I hope I can hold her real soon.

Vanessa: Yes, you will be able to hold her real soon. We will just have to help you for a while. Byron, are you ok with it?   Byron: I'm ok with it. Maybe since we will have a baby around here, she will stay out of my room and leave all my stuff alone (Pointing at Samantha)-Who is now sticking her tongue out at him.

Thank You for Your Service

I remember back when she first came to us as a foster child. Momma Gladys had talked to her contact with Child services about us fostering her. In the beginning, I didn't think it would work. We both had jobs, and with the 2 older kids, having a baby would be a lot of work. Plus, having a foster kid meant people would be in and out of your house a lot, and I wasn't too sure about that. With her being such a tiny baby, I was scared one of the kids would handle her too rough and hurt her. That didn't happen, and they were actually better with her than we thought they would be. Carried her everywhere and didn't want her to cry at all.

The sad thing is, right when we got used to having her, things took a turn, and we were completely thrown off guard. I guess we just got too comfortable with the situation. The kids were at School, and Richard was working. I had just fed Jennifer, and now she was down for her noon nap. I got up to fix a bite to eat and noticed a white car parked outside. At first, I thought it was somebody just parked in the wrong spot like always. Then I saw 2 people getting out of the car and heading towards our steps. Two people, a short, plump man with a big mustache who looked like he had on a bad toupee'. Accompanied by a tall, thin, redhead woman in heels dressed in a plaid skirt carrying a briefcase. I met them at the door, and they asked if Mrs. Vanessa or Mr. Richard were home. I told them I was Vanessa and asked what I could do for them? They immediately presented me with a State ID that suggested they worked for Family Services. The visit kind of surprised me because they usually called before they came. But then I remember when we went through the classes, they mentioned they do pop up visits too. Before I could invite them in, they said they needed to talk to me about Jennifer. I directed them to the living room to have a seat.

Even though I knew this could be a regular visit, for some reason, when they said they needed to talk to me about Jennifer, right then, I got a sick feeling in my stomach. We haven't done anything but loved her. I'm thinking somebody has called in and filed a false report or something. Almost immediately, they calmed my fears and said they had not received any adverse reports to date. They went on to say, as their I.D. suggested, they worked for Family Services but specifically

Children's Services. I was trying to follow to figure out why again they were here. They said they were there to pick up Jennifer. It didn't appear they were going to give me any other explanation. I'm assuming they saw my facial expression of complete shock and went on to explain further. The female, who introduced herself as

Betty Henderson, said a family member had decided to adopt her. She would be placed in their immediate custody until the custody hearing in a couple of months. She said they did have to take some classes and have a Home Study, but she was almost sure they would adopt her without issues. She then went on to say how happy she was when a child is placed back with family. She turned towards me, put her hand on my shoulder, and said,

"Thank you so much, Mrs. Vanessa, for your services. I know you must be so happy that Jennifer will be in her forever home, with family soon."

I immediately looked at Jennifer, and she was still sleeping. The man who introduced himself as Bobby Weathers

stood over her with his hands in his pocket. Actually, I didn't like the way he looked at her. I feel like I don't trust him for some reason. Maybe it's the mustache, man wig, or perhaps just me being overprotective and paranoid. We've had her almost 9 months, and these people waltz in here and say they are here to take her and expect me to just say ok. I gathered myself, cleared my throat, and asked if there was any way we could have the same option to go ahead and adopt her immediately since she's been with us all this time. We are a few steps ahead of them since we have already had our home study, and she is very familiar and happy here. You would have thought I just told her a funny joke. She chuckled and said, "No, ma'am, I'm sorry, that's not how this works. You are lower on the list because you're not a family member. Plus, her mother is white, her family is white, and same-race adoptions are highly encouraged."

She stood up, straightened her skirt, and asked Bobby to go get the car seat. Then turned towards me with a fake

smile and asked if I could be a dear and grab her things. She said they would like to get her to the other family as soon as possible since they have to get papers notarized before 5 pm today. I went to our room and grabbed her diaper bag and basket of clothes I had just washed. I picked out her favorite blanket, smelled it, and put it under my pillow as if I had to hide it from them. I walked as slow as I could back towards the living room. As I turned the corner, the lady was holding Jennifer and placing her in the car seat. Her eyes were open, but she was still very sleepy. I walked over to her and touched her cheek. She looked at me and smiled such a big smile but immediately went right back to sleep. I gathered my thoughts, cleared my throat, and started telling her how many ounces of formula she usually drinks, how often, how to get her to burp, and when she ate last. I tried to tell her what her favorite toy was and how we usually put her to sleep, but she immediately cut me off.

Mrs. Henderson: That's ok I think we can figure all that out without any issues. She told me I would receive a call from

Children's Services soon that will be something like an exit services survey. They would appreciate it if we would participate. She grabbed up the car seat and walked very fast towards the door. Turned around in a flash and asked me if I could open the door for her. When she cleared the doorway, she yelled, thanks again, Vanessa, for your service, but she never even looked at me.

All I could see of Jennifer was her little right foot bopping back and forth to the beat of Miss Henderson's brisk

stride. I watched them place her car seat in the back seat, secure it, then they both head towards the front seats. We never did that. I always sat in the back with her to make sure she didn't choke or anything. I immediately started to cry. I held it together for as long as I could, but reality just hit me. Jennifer is gone and never coming back. It's all I can do to make it to my room, grab her blanket, and cried like a baby. I thought back to the prayer I prayed before we got her. I asked God for her and believed he gave her to us, but how could this happen? I know nobody considers me a "Bible Thumper" or anything, and I knew I had a lot of work to do concerning my mouth at times. Still, my belief in God and faith has always been strong! Until now, that is because I give up. God, how can you let this happen? Why are you punishing us for only trying to fill a void in her and show her love??

> I cried myself to sleep and woke up with a horrible headache. I got up and realized I still hadn't eaten anything and

was feeling shaky. I stumbled to the kitchen and fixed myself a ham sandwich. I took 2 bites and threw it away. I begin to wonder how I'm going to tell the kids and Richard. I didn't have a choice, but I feel like such a failure by letting them waltz in here and take her. I wish I would not have even opened the door.

Permanent

This doesn't happen often. Especially when it's cold. But we had a great day at work. We were ahead and really didn't have a lot to do. My Boss tried to send me home twice, but I needed the money and was off the next 2 days, so I stayed and let some of the younger guys go home. Even though today wasn't that bad, I still couldn't help but wonder what Jennifer has been doing today and if Vanessa got any rest. I know I was worried at first, but everything has been going well. She's sleeping a lot better and smiles all the time. She doesn't fuss much at all.

I'm glad we got her, but I still can't see why her family wouldn't want her. They haven't said anything about her being moved anywhere or anything. I tried to fight the feeling first, but when I get home, I think we need to go reach out to Momma Gladys and see what all we need to do to make sure she never leaves. I was worried about Vanessa at first, but she's got me wrapped around her chunky little finger, and I don't know what I would do if she had to leave.

Samantha and Byron

Samantha:

Jennifer is so cute! I always wanted a little sister but never thought it was a chance I would have one. I mean, I know she won't be my little sister, but I can pretend, and she could be my own live baby doll!! Since she got bigger, Momma let me hold her now. And one time, she even let me help feed her. I don't like to hear her hollering, though. She does that when she gets her diaper changed, and I get sad every time because she will look at me like she wants me to help her. I cry when she cries, but I try to make sure nobody sees me because I, didn't feel like hearing Byron's mouth. He gets on my last nerve. I remember when I was little. I had so much fun. Daddy use to work a lot but he still always found time to play with us. He used to lay on the floor and pretend to give us helicopter rides on his legs. Then sometimes, he would even put me on his shoulders and walk around the house. I hope she stays with us all the time because I can't wait to see him do that with Jennifer when she gets older.

I know Byron doesn't want her in his room, but that's ok because I want her to be in mine anyway. I want it to be pink and purple. She can have the pink side, and I can have the purple one. Or really, she can have whatever side she wants. We can make forts out of blankets, play in makeup, and do each other's hair. Byron is going to be jealous because he won't be able to do that with us. I won't ever let nobody mess with her either. I'm going to be a good big sister, and when she gets older, she can ask me for help with anything. All she got to do is ask.

Byron:

Momma and Daddy are acting like this baby, maybe our little sister soon. I like having her here. I rush home to hold her most days before Samantha can get her. I'm ok with her staying. I've got used to her being here, and I know how to make her laugh so loud. She only does this particular giggle when I tickle her, and I know it makes Samantha jealous.

I just hope she doesn't grow up and act like Samantha. She barely has to do anything around the house. Then, every time I turn around, they are buying her a new dress, fixing her hair, or buying some new shoes. And we fight like cats and dogs. She's the only person that makes me mad real fast. I think because she's so spoiled. I know I'm the oldest, but I have to do way more around the house than she does. Plus, I feel like she gets away with murder, and we shole don't need two Samantha's around here.

I already got it all figured out. When I get older, I'm taking Jennifer with me everywhere I go so the girls can see her

and know I'm a good big brother. I would take Samantha with me too, but she's way too hard-headed, fast and grown for me. Then Momma and Daddy said, I can't hit her or anything, so I know she would act up. The girls think a guy taking care of the baby sister is cute.

I know I talk about Samantha a lot, but I'm going to be a good big brother to her and Jennifer just the same. I know Samantha is always doing something to make me mad, but when my baby sisters get older, aint nobody going to mess with them. Then, if they ever need big brother for anything, all they got to do is ask.

Some Vacation Day

I never took a vacation day, "just because." Normally if I took off I had plans. But I've waited for this day for weeks—Nobody's home except me. I had plans to lay on every piece of furniture I could find and just rest. It sounded good, but sadly, I feel like today is going to be one for the books. It's only a little after ten, and it's already been a bad day for me. Seems like everybody has been getting on my last nerve. It all started when the kids didn't wanna get up for School. Then, Byron couldn't find his homework sheet and Samantha, couldn't find her shoes. Then to top it off, they almost missed the bus. I finally get them on there in time, then not an hour later, I got a call from the School saying they were acting up on the bus. They said they got one more time to have issues this nine weeks and they will be kicked off for the rest of the year. Which is not going to work, since me and Richard work early and won't be able to take them. How do you Live with somebody, leave the house together, and then get into it on the School bus so bad that you're about to get kicked off? I've been as patient as I could be with them, but today I made my mind up, I don't care what Richard say; I'm tearing them up when they get home.

      I finally get all cozy on the couch to watch my show I never get to watch since I'm always working during this time. Not five minutes in and the phone rings. What the hell?! If it's that School, the hell with a whooping at home, I'm gonna get their ass up there. I make it to the phone, and it was a lady on the other end asking for Mrs. Vanessa. Now see, I already know this some mess. I'm about to tell her Mrs. Vanessa has moved.

Vanessa: This is Vanessa

Caller- Mrs. Vanessa, this is Mrs. Betty Henderson from Social services.

Vanessa- Mrs. Henderson, we already did the survey and turned it in.

Mrs. Henderson- Oh, yes I received it. Thank you but I wanted to talk to you about Jennifer.

Vanessa: What do you mean?

Mrs. Henderson- We have Jennifer here, and she is still available if you and your husband are still interested.

Vanessa-Ummmm. What do you mean available if we are still interested?

Mrs. Henderson- The adoption with the family didn't work out, and since any other family members listed have waived their rights to her, then yall are the next ones in line to get her if you still want her.

Vanessa-Is this a joke? Yes ma'am, we do!

Mrs. Henderson- No, this is not a joke and she's all yours if you want her. But maybe you should talk to your husband first before making such a big decision?

Vanessa- Oh...Well, I know what he will say, but I guess I should.

Mrs. Henderson- Ok, sounds like a plan. There is one thing I forgot to mention. She would have to be picked up here at the

Orphanage, which would be about a three-hour drive for yall. . Would that be a problem or deal breaker?

Vanessa: No ma'am it don't matter how far we need to go, just tell us when and where and we will be there.

Mrs. Henderson: Ok good, I will look forward to hearing from you next week sometime with your decision.

Vanessa- Oh, Mrs. Henderson, it will be way before then. He gets off in a couple hours, and we will call you right back. I hung up the phone and had to pinch myself. I had gave up hope a long time ago of ever seeing Jennifer again. I can't count how many nightmares, I'd had, reliving them coming to get her. That day, not only was Jennifer taken from me, but I was stripped of any strength I thought I had. I felt weak, unsure of myself, and a failure to not only myself, but to Richard and the kids. Now Mrs. Henderson is calling saying we can have her back if we want her!! Of-course we WANT HER!!!

I can't wait until Richard gets home. I don't even know how to tell him; he is going to be so excited! I went to our room and pulled out her blanket, baby book, and memory box. Before today it was way too painful to even look through. Richard. Rounded all of them up the next week after she left. I know he looked in the box from time to time because it was moved around a lot. Then I could always tell when he was really thinking about her and I felt like it was always misplaced around those times. I couldn't stand to have them out in the open after she left; I've not looked at them since he put them in there.

As soon as Richard got home, I ran out to the car to tell him about the call with Mrs. Henderson. He was in disbelief like I was. We both sat there and just looked at each other for about ten minutes. Then he said he was ready to go get her. I told him she was in an Orphanage that was about three hours away. I think that made him even more anxious to leave right then and there. I told him I didn't think it would be that easy and we needed to call Mrs. Henderson back and let her know our decision. He wondered why I didn't go ahead and tell her when we talked earlier. I told him I tried to but she pretty much insisted I wait on him to be a part of the decision.

We said then we wanted to wait before we told the kids. We didn't want to get their hopes up and something fall

through. We knew what that felt like and even if we had to face that, we didn't want it for them. We called Mrs. Henderson back and got her answering machine. I left a message for her to call us back but looked at the clock and its 4:52 on a Friday. I could have just melted onto the floor. I know she's probably out of the office until next week. That's probably why she said for us to call her next week with our decision. I'm sure she didn't want to deal with all the paperwork this late.

We were so scared we wouldn't hear from Mrs. Henderson until that next week but she finally called us back later

that night around six. She said she would need to be out for surgery and would no longer be taking care of our case. She said not to worry because she already shared all the information with a co-worker-Mrs. Opal who will be now working our case. She said she is who had been caring for Jennifer, and her office is at the Orphanage as well. She said we could go get Jennifer, that next week. Preferably on a weekday before noon, in case items need to be Notarized. We opted to go as early as we could to get her-Monday.

Road Trip

We told the kids they wouldn't have to go to School on Monday. They were super happy but wondered why. We told them we would be going on a trip to help with another baby. Blank faces across the board. It was obvious they had their guard up, but who could blame them? .They had a lot of good questions. We answered them to the best of our ability and believe it or not, that was the first time we realized the severity of the trauma it caused them loosing Jennifer. I feel so bad that I grieved so much myself, that I didn't have a chance to reach out to them like it's obvious that I needed to have had. The car window had ice all over it. Richard and Byron were outside getting the car ready while Vanessa and

Samantha were still inside getting dressed.

Samantha: It's so early, and I'm so sleepy, Momma. Where are we going anyway?"

Vanessa: We are going to pick up the baby we talked about the other day. We talked about this already.

Samantha: How old is the baby? Is it a boy or girl? ?

Vanessa: We got to hurry; your Daddy will be yelling in a minute. He hates to be late for anything.

(Richard and Byron, warming the car up, checking the oil and tire pressure)

Byron starts asking where they are going and why did they have to be up so early.

Richard: Didn't we tell you all this a few days ago?

Byron: Yeah, but I didn't know it was all happening today. How long does it take to get there? What's the baby's name? I hope they don't come and get the baby like they did Jennifer.

Richard: You are asking way too many questions. Grab that ice scraper and start to clean the window off so we can get on the road. We got a three-hour drive there and back, and I want to make it back before it gets dark.

A few seconds into Byron clearing the window, he turned back around and asked. "But how long are a few hours away?

Richard: Byron, forget the window! Just go in the house and tell them to hurry up.

Richard

I know the kids got a lot of questions and I feel bad for not going into a lot of details today, but my nerves are shot. We are actually going to adopt her. We will be changing her name and everything. I know it may take some time to be 100 percent official, but they say there aren't any family members left to try and get her which was the problem last time.

The drive was pretty smooth. The kids slept most of the time, and the roads weren't that busy. Finally, we pulled up to an old brick building, that looked like it could use some paint, with a huge sign out front that read, "Caring Hearts Foster Home." We walked up tethered wooden steps to the double doors, covered with chipped paint. We rang the doorbell and a pleasant, middle-aged woman answered. We told her we were there to see Mrs. Opal. She invited us in and led us to a small, somewhat scarce space at the end of the hallway. The room was pretty much empty except for a playpen, a desk, and a couple of chairs. We did have a bit of a wait. Actually, I was scared something happened, and this wasn't all going to be able to work out. I could tell Vanessa was getting anxious because she started fumbling through her purse, looking for her wallet, then her medicine. Both of which, she mentioned earlier, she was leaving in the car. Of course, I'm just as nervous, if not more than she is.

A few minutes later, the door opened, and a thin black lady with grey hair in a giant bun walked in with our baby in her arms. She was wearing a pink dress with a hat, wrapped up in a cream-colored blanket. She was sleeping so peacefully, but she has definitely grown a lot over the last couple of months. The lady had a smile on her face when she walked in; I know that made us both feel better. She placed the baby in the playpen, walked over, and introduced herself to us. I wanted to grab her out of the playpen but didn't want to act too anxious and jinx anything.

As soon as she laid her down, the kids ran right over. They stood there hanging over the top of that pen, just staring at her. I'm sure they were wanting to wake her up but didn't. Mrs. Opal reached the desk and pulled out a stack of papers. She went back over her medical history with us. Still, she said she could not share any other details about how she ended up in

Foster care. We didn't mind as long as we could have her back

Mrs. Opal sat down and went over rules, requirements, and told us the process can be nerve-wrecking and take

some time to get through. Of course, we know all this since we went through it with the kids, but still, it's nerve-wrecking to have to wait until it's final to know nobody will ever come back and take her. She mostly talked to Vanessa, so I'll admit, I wasn't really paying that much attention. I kept looking around at the kids and the playpen. I couldn't see Jennifer from where I sat, and it was bothering me. I hadn't looked in her face for months and she's so close I just can't stand not seeing her. My heart started pounding, and I had to stand up and stretch my legs. I walked over to the playpen and looked at Jennifer, who was even more beautiful than I remember. The kids were staring and watching her every breath. I walked back to my seat and grabbed Vanessa's hand.

Vanessa

Richard glanced at me with a huge smile, several times as soon as Mrs. Opal started going over details about the

adoption. But that was short lived because not even two to three minutes after Mrs. Opal sat down in front of us, he jumped up acting like he was stretching and immediately walked over to see Jennifer. I couldn't wait to see her either but stayed seated to take all the information we were being given. I was very anxious, to say the least. Even though I know the information was important, I'll admit, I zoned out for a few seconds trying to listen to Richard and the kids behind me.

We decided not to tell the kids we were getting Jennifer back until after we got here and able to feel the situation

out. I knew it had been several months since we saw her, and I figured she would look different. I just couldn't let my guard down and make the kids have to re-live losing her again if this didn't actually work out today. I took a couple deep breaths and started to re-focus. Mrs. Opal went on to say we would still have home visits and depending on findings, court dates, processing of paperwork, etc. Still, at times, it could even take years to be final. But, she reassured us, as long as we completed all requirements, we didn't have any complaints phoned in on us that were determined to be accurate, etc., then we would pretty much be able to finalize the adoption process. We just have to wade through the process and all the red tape.

Byron and Samantha's New Spark

Samantha: Aww, it's a girl and she's so cute!!

Byron: Yeah, she is.

Samantha: I wonder what her name is?

Byron: I don't know.

Samantha: She looks like Jennifer to me.

Byron: No, she don't.

Samantha: Yes, she do.

Byron: Now you know Jennifer was way littler than her.

Samantha: I know, but that was a while ago, and you know she is bigger now.

Byron: Well, I don't think it's her because this baby's hair is different too. Jennifer's hair was kind of brown looking, and she didn't hardly have any.

Samantha: Yeah, I know that's what I was just thinking too.

They continue to stare at her in amazement. Each was wanting to touch her and Samantha, in particular wanting to hold her. When nobody was looking, she tried to poke her fingers through the holes in the playpen and touch her, but they wouldn't fit, so she just smashed her face on the netting of the playpen and stared at her.

Samantha: I love her, and we are going to be best friends

Byron: Tell me how yall going to be best friends, and she's a baby. That's so stupid. You get on my nerves saying crazy stuff all the time.

Samantha: That's why she's going to be my best friend and not yours because I can't stand you. I'm going to tell her not to even like you because you mean all the time. Then when she gets bigger, we will play together and not talk to you at all. Byron: That's what you think. You don't like me and you probably aint gonna like her either when Momma be loving all on her. You know you liked Jennifer too until she was there for a while.

Samantha: No, I didn't!! I loved Jennifer. I just couldn't play with her much since she was so small. Then they came and got her, and Momma was soo sad. Then that's when I said I didn't like her because I didn't like seeing Momma, so upset. I loved

Jennifer and she loved me.

Byron: Well, I hope they don't come and take her because Momma would go crazy this time.

Reunited

Finally, Richard grabbed her out of the playpen. A small tear ran down his cheek, and he held her close to him. The kids looked so confused. They had never seen him cry. I looked at them and told them this baby was actually Jennifer. I could tell they weren't convinced by the puzzled looks on their faces. I knew Richard wasn't going to give her up anytime soon, so I pried her little arm from him, pulled up the sleeve of her dress to show them her heart-shaped birthmark. I struggled to try to get any other words out but, didn't have to because we were all hugging each other and sharing tears of joy.

We never intended to keep it from them forever. I mean, how could we? There was no way this baby and Jennifer would have the same birthmark. I felt our family was complete; we were just missing that one little piece of paper to make it official. We started kicking all kinds of names around. But for some reason, I keep going back to the first time I saw her at Momma Gladys' in that Jade sleeper. Seeing as how Jade has always been my favorite color, I held onto that as a sign from the very beginning. Then I looked up the meaning and loved it even more. I ran it by the kids and Richard, and they all loved it. We still had to come up with a middle name. Samantha said she liked the name Jewell and I thought that was a great idea.

Jade Jewell Thomas it is!

Part III

Meet Jade

Everything has been going well—Jade's sleeping and eating ok. The kids love her, and she came back and fit right

in. I was convinced the first time her little eyes were able to focus in on all of us, that she remembered us.

Taking care of her and loving her was a piece of cake. The hard part, the one thing we didn't prepare for was all the questions. We go to Church or the store and nothing but looks. They look like they think we've kidnapped her or something. A few times, people would even ask me what she was?? At first, I had no idea what they were talking about; then I realized they were referring to her race. No matter how many times that question was asked, it would piss me off; but most times I did an excellent job of hiding it.

Then one day, I took the kids to the bar-b-que street festival. Richard had to work, so it was just us. It was such a

hot day, but there were several tents and shaded areas, and we took full advantage of them throughout the day. I decided we would grab a bite to eat and find some shade until the sun went down and then head home. The kids ate and then ran over to the water sprayer they had out for all the kids to run through. They were having the time of their lives, and I'm sure the water felt good in the heat. I took Jade out of her stroller for a bit. Her cheeks were rosy, and the little hair she did have was stuck to her forehead in sweat. I took off all her clothes, except her diaper, wet a towel with some cool water, and wiped her down to cool her off. She didn't act like she was too hot or anything, but she sure did smile a lot and perked up after I wiped her down.

I noticed a couple ladies looking over towards us off and on. They looked like they were in an intense conversation, but occasionally they would look over towards us. I glanced over as I played with Jade and smiled. I guess that gave them the sign that I wanted to conversate with them or something because a few minutes later, they walked over and sat across the table from us. They introduced themselves as Brenda and Vickie. I figured they weren't from around here because I had never seen them before. It was apparent early on that Vickie was the "ringleader." She said how cute Jade was, asked me her name and how old she was. I answered her questions, but I started to feel like I was getting the third degree. I started dressing her and called the kids over to start rounding stuff up to head home. We had, had a long day, and I was ready to get home to some air and take these shoes off. I guess after they looked at me and the other kids, they just had to keep pushing. They then went on to tell me how cute all the kids were. Of course, I thanked them and kept tidying up the area to leave. As soon as I stood up, turned and walked away, one of them yelled out, "Oh, I meant to ask you what is she?" Immediately I stopped. I turned around, and Vickie was standing up with her arms crossed, smiling.

Vanessa: Excuse me?

Vickie: I know she aint black, so what is she?

I felt like my head was about to pop off. I can't believe this stranger is all up in my business. Then she was standing there, waiting for me to answer her question. Like she's a teacher quizzing me for a pass or failing grade. I slowly walk back towards her and try to compose myself. But the minute my mouth flew open, I knew it was not going to go well.

And then came the wrath…

Vanessa: Vickie, let me tell you one damn thing. I don't know who you are and why you think it's ok to go around asking dumb-ass, intrusive questions like that. Especially when you out here in this hot ass heat with some corduroy pants and a tight turtleneck that's about to choke yo ass. Then you're, "non-fashion savvy ass," thought it was a good idea to cut the top and make it sleeveless. I've been raking my brain for the last 30 minutes trying to figure out why the hell you thought it was ok to wear that shit in July.

Furthermore, you need to introduce that bushel of nappy ass hair under your arms, with the cheap balls of deodorant in it, to a straightening comb, followed by the sharpest razor on the market. Then you have been flashing the biggest smile all day trying to show off that cheap-ass gold cap. All the while, your mismatched cheap makeup is running all down the side of your face. To make it worse, you got 1000 dollars' worth of gel caked up on that ugly, stiff ass weave ponytail.

Brenda: Wait a minute. I know you didn't.

Vanessa: Don't you say shit! I ain't got on your ass yet but will. You had an excellent opportunity to stay out of this.

Brenda: You think I'm scared of you?

Vanessa: You aint got to be scared of me for me to roast your ass; especially with those husky ass feet that look like you have been stomping out hot coals all day. Or better yet, them sharp, rolled up nappy, edges. Both of yall need to take turns kicking each other's ass for allowing the other one to come out of the house looking like that. Then go find some real friends who are going to tell you how you look before you leave the house and make you change.

And back to you, Miss Nosey ass Vickie. Your sorry ass Momma should have taught your simple ass better than to go around asking people about their kids. You don't worry about who or what she is cause YOU ain't got a damn thing to do with or for her. Just know she's mine and human....Stankin Bitch!

I walked off, knowing this would be a forever, no-win battle. But I took it all out on their ghetto asses, and I feel so good.

Maybe that will help; keep me off somebody else ass for a while.

Carol-New Town, Fresh Start

Bucks Pointe was home, but it sure had a lot of bad memories for me. New Town, new start so I'm looking forward to making good ones here. Sure, I don't know anybody here, but that's not always a bad thing. Just got our little place. A 2-bedroom apartment, furnished and utilities included. It's not all that fancy, but it's cheap, and I don't have to worry about anybody trying to break in because a police officer lives directly across the street. I have to try to get Mercedes and Brian settled in a daycare. I just got to do whatever it takes to keep Social services out of my life. They have already taken one of my kids, and I will be damned if they get their hands on another one.

Right after I moved here, I met Kim. She was my neighbor and pretty cool. She tried to get me a job with her at the meat processing plant, but I didn't have anyone to keep the kids. Ever since my baby was taken, I didn't really trust anyone watching them. We had been friends for a while before I told her about the whole situation with the baby. I left Bucks Pointe to get away from the shame of it all, and being new to Bronsonville Heights, I sure didn't want it to follow me here. But at times, I did want to talk about her. If I never talked about her then, it would be like she never existed, and that was so far from the truth.

Kim mentioned to me that there is a lady named Momma Gladys that always has foster kids. She thought maybe if I talked to her, she may know how I go about looking for her. It sounded like a good idea, but I didn't know this lady. Would she think I was crazy? Would she even talk to me?? After a few weeks, I got up the nerve to walk around to Momma Gladys's house, but nobody was home. I left feeling so empty. I had convinced myself I would leave with some information that could help me, but I think my mind was too ready because now I feel even worse than I did before I came. It took me a few weeks to go back. This time, I saw an older lady sitting in a rocking chair, holding a toddler. I walked up to the yard and opened the gate. A small bell rang, and she was startled. She asked me who I was and asked me what I wanted. I told her I had just moved to town and heard she kept foster kids. Before I could get anything else out of my mouth, she said," No ma'am, I can't take no mo kids right now." I went on to explain to her that I wasn't from Social Services needing to place a child, but I had a child who I thought may have come in contact with her. She told me she hadn't had a white baby in several years. I told her my baby may have only been a couple weeks or months old when she may have seen her. I noticed a kid that looked to be 10 or 12 standing in the doorway.

Again, she said she hadn't ever had a white baby. The child came out the door and said," Momma Gladys remember that little baby was here that time-she looked white?

Momma Gladys: Hush child, and gone on in the house and stay out grown folks business!!

Like I said, ma'am, I ain't never had no white baby, so I can't help you.

Carol: I'm sorry for bothering you ma'am. I turn to walk away. I looked back, and she was watching me intently. I stopped and walked back towards her. I'm sorry, but this may help. I know I'm white, but my baby is biracial. Is there by any chance you may have had a mixed baby??

Momma Gladys: I had a mixed baby, but that was a while ago. I don't know what happened to that baby. I had a baby like that for a while, but them folks came back and got her a while ago. I knew she wouldn't be here long because she was so young. People like to get a small baby. When she left from round here, all they told me is they thought they had family for her, but that was some time ago. All I can tell you is to call the Social Workers and see if they can help you because that's all I know.

Carol: Well, thank you for your help; I appreciate it.

Momma Gladys: uhh huh.

Carol:

I walked down the street trying to compose myself so I wouldn't cause a scene. I know that baby they talked about was her. I could tell by the way she looked when I said she was mixed that she too knew she had to be mine. Mixed baby's' are few and far between now. And with Bucks point being such a large town, it would only make sense that they would send her to a small out the way place like this. I know Momma Gladys, didn't give me no information with her mouth, but her eyes gave me more than enough.

They After the Thomas Baby

Momma Gladys: Vanessa, there was some white lady come around here looking for that baby.

Vanessa-WHAT?!! WHEN??

Momma Gladys-She just left out from round here. She was walking and asked me if I have her baby here or had I seen her baby. I don't know, but it sounds like yalls baby may be hers. I told her I didn't know anything. Just told her the folks came and got her. I just want to tell y'all because she may be asking other people, and then she may show up there.

Vanessa- What am I supposed to do if she comes here?? Aint no way I'm letting nobody in here to take her away again!! We had to wait all them months but the people told me everything was final, but can she get her???

Momma Gladys-Naw Chile, she can't get nothing. That's all over with now. Aint no way she can get that baby.

Vanessa- Whew, thank God.

Momma Gladys- But…. She shole can cause yall some problems.

Vanessa- What do you mean?

Momma Gladys-Even though it's final and yall got her. She can still come around and tell folks y'all got her baby. If I was yall, I would just keep her out from round there.

Vanessa- Lord, what am I supposed to do. We prayed for this baby, and I can't have her come over here and cause problems. What if she tries to steal her? Or tell her who she is when she gets older. She may even tell other people around here that she's her child. I know everybody knows I didn't birth her, but I sure don't feel like all the talk like I stole this woman's baby. Richard said not to worry about it. He said Jade is so young, and by the time she gets up old enough to understand it all, this lady may be long gone. Still, every-time I went to the store, I made it a point to leave Jade at home. I hated to leave her, but I didn't know who the lady was or what she looked like, but I sure didn't want to run into her and have it out on isle 5.

Jade Goes to School

I never went to any School or daycare before I started Kindergarten. I was one of the lucky kids who got to stay home with my Grandmother. I loved it. Every day I played with my dolls, Lilly and Flower Sprinkles, and watched cartoons all day. But, when it was time to go to Kindergarten, I didn't want to go. Then Momma said all the kids my age had to go, or they would put her and Daddy in jail. She said she would let me stay home sometimes, with her when she took off work if I was good.

The night before, I cried, and I couldn't sleep that good. Byron & Samantha had been going to School for a while, and they told me all about it but said they didn't like it and it was hard. Momma and Daddy told me what not to do for the last two weeks. Now, everything started to run together, and I was nervous because of a whole list of stuff like:

1. What if they lose me or I get lost?

2. What if I couldn't remember how to spell my name?

3. What if the teacher was mean?

4. What if the kids don't like me and they talk about me?

The School was nowhere from the house and I had passed it my whole life. It was a small white building with a chain link fence around it. I always stared at the playground on the side of the building. On the first day, Momma walked me into my classroom. A chubby short lady met us at the door with glasses that sat on the tip of her nose. She has chains coming from her glasses and tight brown and white curls in her hair. She walked with a little bit of a limp. She smiled at us, said she was my teacher, and walked me over to a small desk. It had a long slit on the top that had a purple pencil in it. My name was also on a white piece of paper on top of the desk.

I remember that day like yesterday. I had two pigtails with red ribbon, a red dress with white pockets and black patten leather shoes, and white ruffled Bobbysocks. I wanted to play with the other kids, but I had a dress on and those church shoes. I was always a Tomboy at heart. All-day, I kept catching myself sitting like I had pants on and had to remember and hurry up and pull my skirt down. Momma said she thought I would forget I had a dress on, so she made me put shorts on under it. I'm glad too because I saw one of the boys looking at me funny and then I realized he was looking at how I was sitting. I was embarrassed by my knees. They were covered with old and new, scrapes and cuts. Most of them had come from me climbing the big tree in our front yard. Momma hated for me to climb the tree, so I had to do it when she was at work.

She was scared I would fall, but I could climb that tree better than anybody in the neighborhood.

Adopted ?

Thinking back to my childhood, it was pretty average, I would say. Plenty of cousins, making mud pies, building

forts, and adventures. We had a huge backyard, and since we lived with our Grandmother and Grandaddy, everybody always came to our house for Sunday dinner. Those were the best days. Our house was full of people laughing, eating, and gossiping. Sometimes a few of the grandkids would stay the night. We would have a HUGE pallet all over the living room floor. Then, the next morning, Grandmother would cook a big breakfast for all of us, then we would play outside all day. We played in the ditch behind the house most of the time, pretending to fish but mostly looking for treasures instead, finding crawdads.

Everybody in the neighborhood pretty much played in the ditch at some point in time.

One day, when I was seven or eight, I was at one of my cousin's house playing. It was so hot that day, and we had been outside for hours. We usually played well together, but we got into an argument that particular day and started pushing each other. It all started because I was riding his bike, and he wanted it back. Yes, I had a bike, but they had so many there, so I didn't bring mine. Before I could get off the bike, he pushed me off, and I scraped my knee. Afterward, I started crying and shouted I was running home to tell Grandmother. He then went on to say that Grandmother wasn't my Grandmother anyway. He said she was his Grandmother but not mine. I called him stupid and told him to shut up since what he was saying didn't even make sense. If she wasn't my Grandmother, why was I living with her? I turned to run down the street, and he yelled after me, "She aint your Grandmother, she's mine because you are adopted, and I'm not." What did that mean??? We always said mean things to one another when we got mad, but I never heard that word before. I cried all the way home, ran into the house, and busted through the door. I was looking for Grandmother, but Momma came out of her room, grabbed me by my arms, and asked me what happened. I was so mad and upset I could barely get anything out. She looked down at my knee and got even more frantic. She grabbed both my arms and shook me, and said Jade, what is it!! I wiped my face and nose with my dusty hand and told her Brandon had told me Grandmother wasn't my Grandmother.

She calmed down, chuckled, and said, that's crazy, you know she is, and told me not to pay any attention to him. Then told me to go in the bathroom and wash up, and she would put a Band-Aid on my knee. I started to walk towards the bathroom but turned around because I forgot to tell her what he said about being adopted. That's the part that scared me because I didn't even know what it meant. Momma, I was mad at him because of my knee, but he hurt my feelings when he told me I was adopted. I aint adopted, am I Momma? What is that anyway?

Momma stopped in her tracks and turned to look at me. She had a look on her face that scared me, and I didn't

even do nothing. She asked me again what he said. I told her that he told me Grandmother was his Grandmother, not mine, because I was adopted, and he wasn't. I had no idea what that meant, so I asked Momma again what it meant. I had no idea her face could look anymore mad than it already did, but I was wrong. She started towards the kitchen and told

Grandmother. All I could hear was Grandmother saying, "oooohhh now, I know he didn't say that!!

Grandmother came out of the kitchen and met me. She grabbed me and told me not to pay any mind to what any of the kids say. She said they just run their mouth and don't know what they're talking about. She told me I was her Granddaughter, and I should know it because I live with her and we look alike. She hugged me and told me he was probably just jealous. That made me feel good. I always loved Grandmother, and she was right. We were the same color. I remember one time I asked

Momma why I didn't look like her or Daddy, and she told me because I looked like Grandmother, which made sense to me. I don't know why Momma got so mad. All I could hear out of the kitchen was Momma yelling and cussing. I thought she was talking to herself. Then I realized she was on the phone. The last thing I heard her say before she slammed the phone down was, you better tell them to shut their ass up before I shut it for them. I don't know who she was talking to, but I figured it was Brandon's Momma or Daddy.

She walked around the corner from the kitchen and situated her shirt. I could tell she was still mad. The last time I

saw her this mad was when somebody put some white powder in an envelope on our doorstep with a note telling us we needed to move or something was going to happen to us. I still don't know why they put that powder on our doorstep, but Momma said it was some witchcraft mess and not to worry about it. But then I remember Momma talking about it for a long time and said she was laying for somebody to bring their ass back in the yard.

    She told me I didn't have to worry about him repeating it, and if he did, for me to let her know, and she would take

care of it. That made me feel better because he probably ended up getting a whooping, and that will make anybody keep their mouth shut. I went to the bathroom and cleaned up. While I was in there, I remembered that Momma still didn't tell me what adopted meant. Oh well, I'm not, so it don't matter, no way.

Skate Time

I loved playing over at my neighbor Meesha's house. That was the only other house Momma would let me go to other than my cousins' house. I liked going there because I felt like a big girl when we played together. She was two grades ahead of me, but she was always so nice to me. She didn't treat me like a younger kid. I got to go there about once or twice a week since Momma and her Momma were friends. That's how it went. If Momma didn't know their parents or like them, I better not even think about asking. I already knew the drill to make up and excuse why I either didn't want to go or couldn't. Neither of which included, "Because Momma doesn't like your Momma or Daddy." All the girls in the neighborhood wanted to skate at her house because she had a huge concrete driveway. Her Momma and Daddy were pretty much like mine. They wouldn't let any and everybody come over to play if they didn't care for the kid's parents. I'm glad they liked me because they would even move the cars when I came, so we would have more room to skate.

One day Meesha and I were having a great time laughing and playing when her Momma called her in because she had forgotten to wash the dishes earlier. I kept skating since it was still daylight, plus I knew if I went home, I wouldn't be able to come back outside and would have to clean the kitchen myself.

Her neighbor Mr. George was outside washing his car, so I felt safe with him being there. He always watched us while we were outside. Sometimes he even bought us candy and ice cream off the ice cream truck.

It was July and super-hot, but the sun was starting to go down. Since Meesha wasn't going to come back out, I went ahead and took my skates off to walk home. Momma always told me I could come and go to Meesha's house and take my skates, but I couldn't wear them there, or back home. There really wasn't a walkway, and she was scared I would slip and fall in front of a car. I didn't have any shoes, but it wasn't far from the house, so I could walk barefoot that short of a distance. When I stood up and started to walk off, Mr. George called me. I carefully walked over to him because there were tons of sharp, white rocks I had to walk over to get to him. He called me to the back of his car and asked me if I wanted to help him do something and make some money. Money!! Sure. All I could think about was going to the corner store tomorrow with my money buying me a pickle, some penny candy, and a juice. As soon as I made it to where he stood, he stepped into his shed and pulled me in. The hut was open in the front but covered with fiberglass panels on the top and all around the sides. It was so dark in there for it still to be midafternoon. I wondered why we were in there, and he handed me something crumbled up that felt like money. I took it and thought he was walking behind me to turn on a light or something because there was no way we were going to be able to work in the dark.

In a split second, he was behind me. I could hear him but still couldn't make out where he was. I knew there was a light on a string in the shed because I had seen him turn it on before. I figured he was going to grab the string. He loves her, so I know even though I couldn't see anything, I figured he knew just where it was.

A second or row later, the light still wasn't on, and now I could feel him bushing up against my back. Then he whispered in my ear in a gross, rough voice said, "let me play with this." I could feel his body pushing up against my back, but I didn't know what he was talking about because, as I said, I couldn't see. The only thing I could think of him trying to play with was my skates, but I knew he couldn't fit them. Plus, he said he needed me to help him with something, and he was going to give me some money, so none of that made any sense. I felt like my heart started to race because even though Mr. George was there, I was still scared of the dark. I tried to stare long enough for my eyes to focus and see what he was talking about. He smelled like motor oil and sweat. And his breath against my neck was hot and smelled like a cigar.

He grabbed my waist on one side and the rim of my pink shorts on the other. I figure the light wouldn't come on, and he's going to guide me out the shed. Before I could say anything, he put his hands inside my pink shorts and jammed his fingers where I had always been told I better not let nobody mess with.

Just like that, it happened. Everything my Momma had told me about men and boys had just happened. I jerked away, threw the money on the ground, and screamed I don't want it!! I ran soooo fast, barefoot, and forgot my skates. I felt like I was running in slow motion because no matter how fast I thought I ran, I couldn't escape the close sound of his sick evil laugh that sounded like it was right behind me…

I make it to the yard, sweating, heart racing a mile a minute and out of breath. My only goal was to get in the house,

lock the door and get to the bathroom. I bypassed Momma in a hurry. She yelled, what's wrong and all I could get out was the bathroom. I got in the bathroom, locked the door, and just stood leaning with my back against the door, and my arms stretched across it as if that would keep him out. I stood there for a couple minutes and felt numb.

Then the pain between my legs brought me out of my stupor. I was scared to pull my shorts down for fear of what I might find. I walked over to the toilet, pulled my shorts and panties down, and sat there.

I was staring at what was once my favorite pair of shorts and the seat of my unicorn panties stained with blood. I

was scared too, but I grabbed some tissues and attempted to wipe myself. Again, it was painful, so I just patted down there. I pulled the tissue up slowly with my eyes squinted shut. I opened my eyes and looked at the blood-soaked tissue. I wiped three times more before the bleeding stopped. Each time I wondered where the blood was coming from, but then I remembered when he put his hands between my legs, feeling his sharp nails, and realized he must have scratched me when he went in with so much force. I flushed the toilet, and there was a knock on the door. I almost jumped out of my skin!! I sat there, not saying anything.

Momma: Jade, are you ok???

Jade: Yes ma'am!! I'm fine; I'm just going to take a bath because it was so hot out there, and I almost didn't make it to the bathroom in time because I held it too long.

Momma: Ok, well, don't be too long, the foods almost done.

Jade: Yes, ma'am

I sit there in the bath, and all I can think about is Mr. George and how now I'm not ever going to be able to play at Meesha's again.

He used to be so nice, so I can't believe he hurt me like that. I hope he don't ever try to pull Meesha in that shed and hurt her like he did me. I wanted to tell her and my Momma, but I knew I couldn't tell nobody since it was my fault. I should have known better than to go in that shed. In all of 30 seconds and at the innocent age of 8 years old, my relationship with men would never be the same. I felt so stupid because I should have known better.

Missing Pieces

When I was younger, I always made it a point to befriend those who most wouldn't want to be seen with,

much less

call them friends. I never liked animals, but some would say it's like always wanting to mend a broken animal. The funny thing is, I feel I'm the one I'm trying to fix. It's almost like I have to prove I'm a good person. Not sure why I feel the need to crave validation from other people. I feel like I have to prove to everyone I'm a good girl. I hate my skin tone because I can't tell you the number of times, I've heard that I must be conceded or think I'm cute. All that bothered me so. Bad that most times I was never able to accept compliments. Then felt strange wearing makeup-like I needed to dim my own light. It was so bad I even avoided mirrors at all costs. Anytime I glanced in the mirror, If felt like I wasn't supposed to be looking at myself.

And why does she have to prove she's a good daughter friend, girlfriend and all-around good person??

Yeah, I've made my share of mistakes, but I mean everybody does. Nobody's perfect, and I'm not claiming to be; I

keep telling myself that but the worry never goes away. It's like a strange feeling that I don't belong. Even when I'm laughing and Feel I'm in a good place, that little feeling creeps in from the pit of my soul like a reoccurring nightmare. It's like a gnawing ache; Not a pain, but an almost nervous feeling. Like when you're watching a scary movie and feel like something terrible is about to happen. My biggest fear is being abandoned. It's like it's deep rooted inside me.

    I guess I could describe it as feeling like something is missing. Like I'm a puzzle, and there is a piece or two missing. The funny thing is, I have no idea why I feel this way or how I can figure it out.

    My family is great. I'm not worried about anything, but no matter how hard I try, this feeling continues to display its ugly head. Most times, I wonder if it's because of the whole ordeal with Mr. George. Yea I was super young when it happened, but after that day, I never felt comfortable around any boy or man. I was always on edge, but especially if I was in close quarters with them or in a room alone with them. Even though I didn't go back and play at Meesha's house anymore, I still saw Mr. George from time to time. Passing by my house when he was heading home mostly. I always turned my head, but he made it a point to always drive by slowly and blow his horn. I was still too embarrassed to tell anybody about that day. It's funny how something that happened in a two-to-three-minute timeframe can change your whole life. How that situation, even though it's such a small timeframe, can still overshadow many happy childhood memories in a way.

Nichelle

Nichelle is my best friend. We met in Mrs. Wright's 3rd-grade math class and have been best friends ever since.

Nichelle had just moved here from Bucks point. It's bigger than Bronsonville Heights and kind of more like City life. Everybody who moves away moves there. Her Grandmother had passed away, so she and her Momma moved back to help with her Daddy afterward. Nichelle said it was because her Momma felt guilty for not being around when her Grandmother was sick.

I hate why she came, but I sure am glad she did. I remember the first day she walked into class with her two short afro pigtails and pink dress. She had on a necklace, sparkly bracelet, earrings, a pair of white shoes with a small heel, and a shiny bow on top. Her whole outfit was super cute. She came into the room and sat by me. I want to think she chose to sit there, but that was the only seat left. She sat down and smiled. I waved shyly and smiled back. I was happy to have a girl sitting by me since all day I had to sit between Morris and Kylan, who took turns blowing spit wads and pulling my hair. Nichelle was quiet pretty much all morning. Later that afternoon, it started to rain, which meant we had to have recess in the classroom. I asked her if she wanted to play 7UP, and I guess you can say the rest is history. Her sense of fashion is still on point, and we've been inseparable ever since.

Surprise Guest

I can't let her know that she's not mine. I mean she is mine. I can't let her know she didn't come from me. People do this all the time, and some are ok with disclosing all the details, but I can't. I feel like a failure in a way by not having a child of my own. It's funny though because I don't know how much closer or connected to her, I could be. I remember when they came and took her away from me. I thought my life would end that very moment. That was not part of the plan. And I couldn't do anything about it. Richard couldn't either. He's always been a fixer but that he couldn't. I always say it was a God thing us getting her back. As quick as they came to take her, after the court date they mentioned, it was just as fast that they called us and said we could have her. I started to wonder what happened but then me and Richard said we were going to leave well enough alone and just be happy we got her back.

I think that's why she's so special to me because she almost wasn't ours at all. Then there's this lady who had moved

to town a few years back. She went straight to Momma Gladys house asking about Jade. Of course, Momma Gladys didn't tell her nothing. I'm guessing since she didn't, she did her own little investigation because it wasn't too much longer when she showed up at our house.

I invited her in because I didn't want to make a scene. Plus I had to feel her out and didn't want to start out making

her mad. She came in, brought her a couple toys and asked me a lot of questions, like how she ate and if she slept good. Then she wanted to see her. I stayed as calm as I could because I figured Jade was too young to remember her coming by anyway. But right before she left she said she would stop by from time to time to see her. I Ok'd her right on out the door. Then the minute she left, I said to myself she better not bring her ass back. Richard was so scared of what I may do so he said he thought it would be better if we went by her house and all had a sit down. I was ok with that because I honestly didn't think I could compose myself if she came back to the house.

First off, I didn't want her there for no other reason than, just because; which for me was reason enough. But to be

honest, I didn't want nobody to see here coming or going. I mean how would that look?? People already been talking and that wouldn't do nothing but make it worse.

I know Richard got sick of me talking about it all night, but I think that's the only way I could stay sane was to talk

myself through it. We decided we would go the next day and talk to her about the whole situation. I went in trying to be as nice and cordial as I could be. I tried to talk to her like she had some sense, until I realized she didn't have none. She went against everything we said, like she didn't realize how hard this whole thing was on us and could be on Jade when she got older. She started saying she was her kid and she pushed her out so I couldn't tell her when and if she could come see her.
Why she thought to pull that card, I have no idea. But let's just say she put that bad boy right on back up. I matter of fact like told her the most she better ever do is watch from afar but that's it. If Jade gets older and chooses to

seek her out because she heard something, then it's up to her but that the only way she better say anything more than Hi to Jade. And last but not least she better not show up at our house again.

I'm sure she was thrown off because I was very polite when she came by the house because she really caught me of guard and it was just me and Jade there so I didn't want to make a scene but I had to gone jump funky with her that day. It worked too because she straightened right on up.

Now all these Years later, I've been hearing she's going around town telling people Jade's hers. I don't believe that to be true but I don't want to cause any ripples so I'm going to do whatever I need to do, to shut her up. She has a few kids of her own so why would she want to try and cause problems with us I'll never know. Not to mention people are talking. People I've known my whole life occasionally mention that she looks like her other kids too. I don't know if it's her, but I can't take any chances.

I don't know if it's her, but I can't take any chances. Whatever it takes for me to keep her mouth shut, that's what I'll do. At first, it was a place to stay. Then it's 50-100$ here and there. Then she sent the other kids over to ask. All was well until one afternoon someone knocked on the door. I walked towards the door, but Jade was closer than I was. She looked out the glass and said it's the little boy from down the street with a puzzled look. I went to the door and tried to shield her, but she wasn't moving, and he couldn't take his eyes off her. I looked at him the way I always had...with pity.

He stood there with mangled unkempt hair. Worn jeans, tennis shoes that were noticeably too big for him and extremely dirty. His skin had the appearance of mocha, but I had always wondered if some of it was because of poor hygiene or lack thereof. He gave me a note that read, money for food.

Something went all over me until I looked back at him. He does look as if they may truly need the money. I tried not to show my frustration, smiled, and walked off to my purse that was sitting on the kitchen table a few steps away.

I balled the note up while walking to my purse, went in my wallet, and without counting, I gave him what it took for him to go away. Money!! I don't even know how much I gave him.

All I can think about is, that was too close for comfort

    I closed the door and tried to answer the questions she had on her face before she even asked.

Vanessa: I feel so sorry for them. They don't have a lot, and I help them out from time to time. They do always pay me back, that's why I don't mind.

Jade: Yeah, I feel sorry for them too because they really do look like they need the help. I see them from time to time, and they always look so dirty.

Vanessa: She bought it. It worked this time, but eventually, she's going to start asking questions that I don't have the answers to. I've got to get this straightened out before a close call like that happens again.

Jade

I walk through the house reading my favorite book. Samantha and a couple of our cousins were all huddled up in

the back room talking. When I walked through the door, they look up like they thought I was somebody else, and they got caught. I turn to walk back out, but they stop me. It's ok; you can stay. I'm not so sure I want to, but I don't want to seem rude. I keep reading my book, not interested in what they're talking about at all. Just then, one of my cousins turns to me and says, "You know you're adopted, right ?"

    Adopted that word again. I haven't heard or thought of that word since I was eight years old. I didn't know what it meant then, but I do now, and it just hit me like a ton of bricks. Of course, I don't want them to think I'm bothered by it. At this point, I'm whole-heartedly accepting it to be true.

I glanced up from my book and said yeah, I know. Talk about the look of defeat. She thought she was telling me something. Well, she did, but I wasn't going to give her the satisfaction of knowing she did. She goes on to say yeah, I remember when they got you. I remember when they got all y'all. Why has my world just shifted? This very second. Everybody and everything I've known to be true is a lie. I think back to that day when I was 8. I feel those same emotions today!! I go to my room, locked the door, and cry. Partly because I felt betrayed, but mostly because my entire life, the people I love with all my heart have all lied to me. The family has always surrounded me, but at this point, even though the house is full like always, I couldn't feel more alone.

Unanswered Questions

Since it's apparent that I am adopted, questions are bouncing all around in my head. Where did I come from? When? How did I end up here, and why haven't I been told this? I mean, this is pretty important information to have left out. There were so many times when I walked into an unfamiliar room or was introduced to someone and got funny looks. You know the kind of looks where people are stealing exaggerated stares as soon as you turn your head. Like they are attempting to freeze-frame, a mental picture of you to re-evaluate and process at a later time. Most times, I knew what they were thinking, so I'll admit on several occasions, I turned my head to allow them the time they needed without feeling awkward. It also helped me since I felt like if I looked directly at them, it would give them an inkling that I may be ok with having the whole what race are you conversation. Which was wayyyy far from the truth. I avoided it like the plague.

It's been plenty of times where it felt like people may have even had a preconceived impression of me before even allowing time to really get to know me. If that wasn't bad enough, the most asked question, from as far back as I can remember, is, "What are you?" The dreaded question, a lot of people ask and think is appropriate, but in my opinion, outright rude! Not sure why anybody has to know, or why they think it's ok to ask? Why does it even matter? Due to my fair skin, I got asked that daily. I've always answered black with certainty, but now I'm not only wondering what I am, but who?? That's the last thing I remembered pondering over before I went to sleep and the first thing I thought about when I open my eyes. I woke up when it was still dark and overtly quiet. Like when all you hear, no matter how hard you try, is a faint buzzing sound. I lay there with my eyes wide open as if I'm going to think this whole thing was a dream that I'm still in. But it's not.

I'm still in my clothes and shoes from the night before and slept on my book. I must have slept soundly because I don't think I even changed positions. Which doesn't make sense because I still feel so drained. I lay there and just think. It's amazing where your mind can take you. I replayed the earliest memories I could remember. Like when I was little, and the white lady came to the house the time. When her and Momma were talking about how I sleep and what I eat. And then she gave me those toys to play with. Now I really want to know who she was? Then I remember being really small and Daddy rocking me back and forth in a blue plastic chair in the living room. I remember laughing so hard. I couldn't have been any more than, maybe two. Which meant my sister and brother should know something too since they are so much older than me.

> Walking down memory lane for what felt like five or ten minutes must have been way longer than that because

before I knew it, it was after eight. I get out of bed and head into the bathroom. I looked in the mirror, and no other way to describe it than looking like a mess. Eyes puffy and red, hair was all over my head. I lay in the bath for what felt like an hour or so. Sitting and thinking until somebody jiggled the handle. Then I heard Momma say, "Jade, are you in there?" Yeah, it's me. I'll be out in a minute. I remember thinking, I hope I sounded normal. I don't want her to know I've figured out the huge family secret EVERYONE has kept from me for the last 12 years.

I've got to ask her when I see her. I'm going to look her in the eyes and bring it up. It's been 12 years. I'm sure she

has prepared for this day since day 1. I do have the right to know my story. Who in their right mind, wouldn't want to know who they are? Whose kid am I? A family friend's? Was I abused and taken by the state and ended up here? I know she has to know. I finish up in the restroom, throw on a T-shirt and some sweats, pull my hair back in a ponytail, and head towards the kitchen on a mission. Of course, like always, Grandmother has cooked a large breakfast, and it smells so good. I fix my plate, but I can't help but pick over my food. To make matters worse, I heard Momma walking up behind me. She put her hand on my back as she walked by and asked if I slept good. My gut dropped, and the hair on the back of my neck stood up. I spoke back, looked up at her, and immediately looked back down at my plate. She sat down, and I cleared it in 10 seconds flat. My goal was to finish so I could go back to my room before we started having our normal gossip session. I had worked my nerve up to talk about it, but now I don't feel like approaching the situation. I just can't. She looks so happy. I can't hurt her by bringing it up. I had no idea how to start that conversation out anyway. The last time I mentioned it, she exploded. Which led me to believe I wasn't. Come to think of it; Out of all that, I don't ever remember her saying I wasn't. She kind of tip-toed around the question then, So why would I waste my time re-asking her the same question and surely get the same answer? Then, there was no way I could ever hurt her like that. Momma loves me, and I love her. I can't see any other way blood could make us love each other any more than we do. Even though my heart aches for the answers I don't have, I can live with it. Whatever it takes for her to be happy. I would never want her to think, me asking who my biological Momma was or where I came from was a slap in the face. I've seen her hurt before, and it killed me. I would never want to cause her any pain if I can help it?

Daddy's Girl

Me and Momma were close, but truth be told, I've always been a Daddy's girl. He could never do any wrong in my eyes. Even though Daddy was out of the house a lot-working. He still made it a point to be the perfect Daddy. I would wait up for him to come home from work but then would lay on the living room floor and pretend to be asleep. Without fail, He would pick me up and tuck me in. I know he had to be tired. He worked 2 jobs Mon-Friday and cut yards on Saturday. But he still did it. That's part of the reason he has Always been my Hero. Stern but fair. Of course, I can't remember ever getting a whooping by him.

    Momma, on the other hand, didn't play, and I didn't try her. She was fair but very strict. I can't ever recall being

disciplined for no reason, but the one thing I didn't like is how strict she was. I couldn't go anywhere. So frustrating to have to make up every excuse in the book as to why you can't go where everybody else is going. As I got older, I was teased relentlessly about it. I know she only wanted the best for me and was determined to keep me on the straight and narrow.

Sadly, I must admit sometimes, that is what made me rebellious in a way.

Crush

Nichelle: Jade, girl, I think he likes you!! Never mind, scratch that; as a matter of fact, I know he does. Every time I go to lunch, he's always asking me where you are, and Friday, he asked me were seeing anybody. I just know he's going to ask me for your number soon, and I'm not going to know what to tell him.

Jade: Don't tell him anything.

Nichelle: What do you want me to do? Just sit there when he asks like I didn't hear him?

Jade: Yep, that'll work. Lol.

Who am I kidding? I see the way he looks at me, and it's been like that for months now. In the beginning, it was straight-up creepy. Lately, though, it's been kind of cute. Especially because I hear other girls talking about him; then to know he's interested in me, I feel kind of special in a way. I haven't been around him that much, but the few times I have been, I can tell he has a great personality and super funny.

> Deon Mitchell sets the bar high in a way; Football star and all-around cool guy; Definitely, a lady's man who had

the perfect smile and a chiseled body to go with it. He could charm the best girl out of whatever he wanted, and believe me, that was a common occurrence. Even Though he was so outgoing, he still has a little bit of mystery about himself.

There are several girls that like him, and I'm sure he flirts, etc., but for now, he seems to be interested in me.

I've not had a real boyfriend to this point, and it's kind of scares me. Only because I know one day soon, we will run into each other alone, and I'm not going to be able to get away without possibly being a victim of his charm. The problem is I have NO IDEA how to talk to a guy. I've been around my cousin Meko a lot, and she's great at it. Me, on the other hand when someone of the opposite sex speaks to me, I get so nervous that I shut down. I know I'm only 13 and expect that to get better, but what am I supposed to do between now and then.

I think Nichelle can tell, too, because I'm always asking her if he was at any event she may have gone to. I try to

slick the question in on her, but she knows me like the back of her hand, so I know she has to know. Heck, I may as well just come out and tell her. I will admit, it makes me nervous that I have these feelings for him. I haven't had a real boyfriend, I just don't want to embarrass myself and stumble over my words or anything.

The Grove

Nichelle goes on and on about what she's going to wear to the Grove next weekend. She went on and on about how she's bought some hot pink and black biker shorts that she can't wait to put on. She then goes on to tell me what went on there yesterday. She has always been the best at telling a story. She is very dramatic and does not leave any detail out, and that's exactly how I like it!!

The Grove was the place to be on Sundays. Any and everybody was there. People put on their best outfits, sat around, and mingled. The guys typically played basketball but mostly stared at the girl they would make their move on for the weekend. It was always so hot and no shade except where the guys normally stood and leaned against the building, but nobody seemed to mind. It was expected, so everyone dressed accordingly. I went a couple times, or should I say, did a walkthrough. Every now and then, I was allowed to go walking with my sister, and we would stop by there for a minute or two. Really, just long enough for me to wish I could go EVERY Sunday.

S since I'm well aware that won't happen anytime soon, for now, I'll just keep getting the blow by blow from Nichelle. Who had on what, who talked to who? WHO's crushing on who. I tried to act uninterested, but this was truly the highlight of my Monday. She knew Momma was strict, but I still tried to act as if I just didn't want to go because it was so hot and I had asthma as a kid, I told her it to use to act up in the Summer, so I have to limit my time outside in the heat and around grass, etc. I'm sure she knew the real reason, but she played along.

We walk down the long hall from Algebra and head to the gym. I hated having to dress out. I always felt like I looked awkward. I felt my thighs were jiggly, my butt stuck out, and my chest was getting bigger by the minute. No matter what bra I wore, I felt like I didn't have good support. I didn't want to walk around and draw attention to myself, but I kind of didn't have a choice. I felt like we all did in our hot pink tee's and tight black shorts, that no matter what, crawled up our thighs.

If tall hat wasn't bad enough, Kendra Russell was in my class and it's very obvious she would rather be doing anything else but sharing the same oxygen as me. I honestly don't know what her deal is with me now. When we were younger. Believe it or not, this whole back and forth started a few years back when we were in Elementary School. She got mad because I didn't pick her to be on my kickball team. I didn't really know her that well because we weren't in the same class and it was between her and Nichelle. Of course, I was going to pick my friend over her. She later told somebody she thought I had it out for her because she thought I said something about her at the end of the game. She said she had tried to be friends with me a couple times, and I always ignored her efforts. I honestly don't know how she figured that? I tried to be cordial from time to time, but it seems like she would then make it a point to throw in a slick jab.

Still, I spoke to her every time I saw her, but she never really initiated any conversation with me.

Later, word around School as she was mad that I got picked to be in the Miss. Sweetheart pageant, and she wasn't. Even though she spent a lot of time working on her race to get added to the ballot. My name was placed on the ballot as a joke by Nichelle. I didn't even want to do it. I tried everything I could not do it and would gladly have let her have my spot without a doubt. I didn't like stuff like that, mainly because I never wanted a lot of attention on me, and of course, being in a pageant, there would be. I remember going dress shopping with Momma. I was so indecisive. It took hours to decide between 3 dresses. I finally decided on a blue and silver fitted, strapless dress. The deciding factor was the time crunch. That particular one fit and did not need any alterations. It was beautiful, but I felt too revealing in a way. As hard as I tried to hide my body at times, there was no hiding in that dress. The bottom was fitted, my hips had started to spread, and my backside was definitely more pronounced here lately. I felt like I was ok with it when I looked in the mirror, so if I could stand on the stage and the curtain comes up, I think I would be ok, but that would not be the case. When we did a run-through, each one of us had to walk directly out on the stage, several different times. Which would mean there would be a side and a back shot!!

Why didn't I just outright refuse...I know it's because Momma always wanted me to be in pageants. For all she's

done for me, I can suck it up and do this for her.

I didn't win, thankfully. I did ok with my talent. I sang a slow ballad that didn't require very much vocal range. I was able to sing with my eyes mostly closed, and that helped a lot. Plus, my ole Elementary music teacher had practiced playing for me, and I was confident she would follow me if, in fact, I sang too slow or too fast.

The talent section was one thing, but in the question and answer section, I completely bombed!!

Question from the panel: What do you think is your best attribute and why?

Jade: Ummmm...I Um would have to say...My eyes

Oh, yea, my eyes because they are brown but sometimes when the light hits them just right, they look Hazel, and a lot of people are buying and wearing hazel contacts now since it's the in look, but I don't have to because mine already look hazel.   WHAT THE HECK WAS THAT?!! I'm laughing at my own self inside, and the same time, absolutely embarrassed!! If all that wasn't enough, out of all the times I walked on this stage, this time I locked eyes with Kendra Russell, who clapped and even gave me a standing ovation as if to say bravo, dumb BITCH!!

Definition of True Love

See there's this guy....Deon Mitchell. My heartbeat for the last couple years. She hates him and I'm not sure why because he never did anything to her. His only crime, if any, was liking me. From the first time, she heard mention of his name she frowned and went on to say how she felt he was bad news. It didn't help when I thought I was sneaking on the phone with him and she was listening in the back room and heard him ask me when we were going to be able to have our first kiss. Not long after that, she dared me to have anything to do with him. Of course, that did nothing but make me want to give him a chance to prove her wrong.

How could somebody who looked at me the way he did ever do anything to hurt me? It's like he needs me to even exist. I feel so secure when I'm with him. Like if anything ever goes wrong, he will make it right. Plus, he's committed to prove her wrong. He says all the time, he can't wait to treat me like a Queen so she will finally realize how much he truly loves me. I feel the same way because I know that's all it will take for her to see what I see and that this is true love if I ever seen it.

My Sweet Jade

Man, my sweet Jade is my drug. The blood that runs through my veins and the air I breathe. I can't explain it, but

she has this thing. I can't put my finger on it, but it sucks you in. It did me anyway. She got, a nice shape, olive skin, a few freckles below her eyes, hazel eyes, a round face and sandy hair. She's shy and careful but she's got in in her. She turns the eye of guys and girls. The guys want to be with her ,and the girls want to know as much as they can about her.

We've been together for 4 years. Four whole years of me putting in much work, that is. She made me wait a year before we could even kiss and another 2 before she let me touch her anywhere else, and four before we made it official. Even though she was far from sexual, anytime I was in her presence, sex was always on my mind.

We've had some ups and downs over the years. I mean who doesn't have issues from time to time? Thankfully we

always made up and still rocking and rolling regardless. I'll admit, I do have one small problem. Everybody asks me If I love her so much, why do I constantly cheat. To be honest, I don't even know myself. I mean I do get off on seeing how many girls I can hook up with. There's not a man around who wouldn't take something that's right in his face.

Then it's a win, win because they aren't going to say anything because they know me and Jade been together, and

they would look like the homewrecker in the end. It's pretty much like, I do enjoy the crave of the hunt. Then knowing that each one of them is going to go above and beyond to try and impress me sexually. Sometimes it really trips me out how they try to show me what they got or can do that they think Jade can't. What they don't know is, Jade doesn't have to do all that and I still ain't going nowhere. I think they are just as curious to see what keeps her around after all this time and I make it a point to not only show them but show them well!!

I mean I do have needs. I played around with a lot of females. It was easier for me to get some alone time with

them. Jades mama is super strict. She can't go anywhere and for whatever reason, she hates me. Maybe she knew from the beginning what I wanted to do to her daughter, lol! Naw but for real I want her. All of her. Not just like a booty call deal. I can see myself with her forever.

I just can't figure out why I know she's enough and everything I want, but I just can't walk the straight and narrow. I'm always messing up and getting caught. Seems like everybody's out to get me. They tell her everything. It's like she got eyes anywhere I go. She doesn't ever get out of the house but can give me blow by blow on all my mess ups. Her girls are on me. And I'm sure the dudes do too. They just sit back waiting for me to mess up. But I ain't worried about that because they going to have to go through me to get her and I don't see that happening.

We broke up a hundred times but always get back together. I just fear one day my begging and pleading won't get

her back and she will end up leaving me for good and that will kill me. I know it will be my fault and I'm trying but it's something in me that always messes up. I take pride in knowing I was her first. I'll never forget that night. How can I forget. She made me wait four years. She had told her Momma she was going to the movies with her cousin. Instead, we met up over my house. Everybody was gone out of town, so I had the house to myself. She came in and was so timid. It was almost like she didn't know me. We really haven't been around each other much alone. I convinced her to come to my room, had on my best cologne and r&b mixtape and the rest is history. We had talked about it a lot, kissed and played around some but I almost couldn't believe it was happening and I straight up cried....

Still, after all I've done my biggest fear is losing her for good. I still get in a rage when I even think about her talking

to anybody else. If that happened, I don't know what I would do. I know she loves me so I doubt that would happen, but you never know when some trifling ass dude may come along and at least try.

I'll admit, she got a mental hold on me. I can't eat or sleep if she's not talking to me. I know we're going to get

married one day and maybe then I'll settle all the way down. But until then, I'll keep creeping and loving me some sweet Jade.

I've been living so careless and 99% of it, revolves around Deon. He's like a drug. I know I don't need him, but I can't leave I'm alone. We've been dating for a little over 4 years, and probably broke up 500 times. In my young mind on one hand I feel like he loves me sooooo much!! He takes so many chances to be with me. Since I can never get out the house, at least four to five times a night from midnight until around six am we play-house. I promise in the beginning I was so scared and didn't want to let him in but he kind of twisted my arm. Then it was pretty much no turning back from there. I couldn't believe he was willing to put his life in danger just to stay with me.

He would never let anybody hurt me. He's my protector and acts like I'm his whole world. On the other hand, I know he's been messing around with other girls behind my back; on more than one occasion that is. Too many to count actually. I know it's crazy, but I think that's one of the reasons I won't leave him alone. I feel we both have a hold on each other in a way. Him because he's the bad boy that I've been dared to date. Me because I know he has some weird attachment to me and to be honest, I like the attention. I will admit, it's been times, that this whole love affair, has been like a game of tug a war. I know he does have some good attributes and I feel in time things will change for the better. Plus, I know there are some girls who are just as intrigued by his bad boy persona and waiting to snatch him up. Since I really can't get out the house at all I take pride in knowing, even though he has been unfaithful at times, he's not going to do anything in my face and he's definitely not going anywhere until I let him.

Better Take a Test

It's getting harder and harder for me to get up for School. This Junior year is really starting to get to me. For the last couple weeks, I been absolutely dragging. A couple times I even fell asleep in class. And don't mention my grades. They are so far from where I want and need them to be. I got to stop all this late night talking on the phone and letting Deon in. All that plus working, I don't have any time for myself. Nichelle said I need to stay the weekend at her place so I can actually get some rest. I think I may take her up on that if Momma will let me.

Alarm clock goes off @ 0605. I reach for the snooze button but, instead, I accidently knocked the clock off my nightstand. Of course, it's still buzzing and getting louder and louder. Do I just lay here and try to tune it out for a few more min of sleep? Or do I get up, hit snooze and get a few more min in. I decide on the latter because, I know for sure I won't oversleep. I jumped out of bed and the min I stood up, I felt extremely nauseated. I tried to cover my mouth with my hands but warm, vomit poured out and around my fingers. I looked down and pretty sure, I saw everything I ate last night. I immediately felt better, but seeing all the chunky vomit, grossed me out so much so that I threw up again. This time it was more like dry heaving and followed by some yellow liquid that spewed out my nose. This has never happened to me. What the hell is going on?!!

> Aw shoo! I bet the pizza we ate last night gave me food poisoning. I remember after I ate a couple slices, I started

feeling like I needed to burp and then my chest started burning. I think something was wrong with the meat or something because that's never happened to me. I wonder if Nichelle's stomach is bothering her. I feel dizzy after all that, but I make It to the bathroom, clean up and get ready for School.

> School went fine and I didn't get sick again but that may be because I didn't eat anything at lunch. Thank goodness,

because If that happened at School, I would be so embarrassed. All day I drank water, chewed gum, and ate some mints I found in my bag. I love my job at the afternoon daycare, and I've never called in, but I don't think I can make it today. I'm so weak. I'm sure because I haven't eaten all day and as of now, all I want to do is go home and go to sleep.

> As soon as I get home, Daddy said he could take me to work when I was ready. I told him I was tired, and they had

too many workers scheduled so they said I could stay home. Momma asked me why I thought, I was so tired. I told her I been up studying late trying to get my grades up before Semester tests. I definitely wasn't going to tell her it's because, Deon been over here 3 times this week. And of course, when he's here, there's not much sleeping happening. I go straight to the room and lay across the bed. My breasts feel a little sore so to top it all off, I'm about to start my period. At least, I will be able to get some sleep this week. I get all comfy and cover up with my fuzzy blanket then bam, I get to pee. Damn! Why didn't I use the bathroom when I first got home? I grabbed a pad from under the sink before I sat down because, I knew when I wiped it was going to be some blood on the tissue. To my surprise it wasn't. Either way I know I'm about to start because my breasts only hurt when I'm about to come on. I finished up in the bathroom but went ahead and put on my pad in case I come on while I'm sleep, then back to sleep I go.

The next day, I get up for School and feel so refreshed. I turned on my Radio, sang and danced to every song
> while

getting ready. I head to the bathroom and again, nothing on my pad. Oh well, I feel so good today that actually makes me feel better that I don't have to deal with that today. I glanced in the mirror and even felt like my eyes didn't look as tired today so that sleep did the trick.

Before I can head out for School, Deon called and said he wanted me to meet him by the flagpole before School

starts so we can talk. I agreed and once, I made it to School, there he was sitting on the bench beneath the flagpole.

Immediately he started right in. He said, he hasn't been able to spend much time with me and he's starting to feel like I been kicking it with somebody else. Boy if he only knew. All I been kicking it with is my bed, every chance I get. I just looked at him. Of course, that pissed him off because he said I act like I didn't care so it must be true. All I could think about was I didn't hear from him at all last night, so I know his ass was up to something and trying to turn it all around on me. I'm not falling for it, though. My day is starting out too good and I'm not going to let him ruin it.

I told Deon, I think we just need to break up. I told him he didn't trust me and I sure as hell don't trust him. I'm

tired of always having to plead my case to you when I haven't done anything. I take his letterman jacket off and push it into his chest. He grabbed my arm and pulled me close to him. Whispered in my ear in a growl. You aint ever going to be done with me. If I ever found out, you been with anybody else I'll kill both of yall. I jerked my arm from him, walked away and laughed. I knew that would piss him off. At this point I'm just trying to act unbothered. I know he won't do nothing to me, but it does make me nervous that if he ever heard anything, he would for sure try to take out whoever the guy is. Of course, I'm not planning on doing nothing, but anybody can make up something and his ass will believe it. Or if he sees me talking to somebody and thinks it's more to it. I just wish he wasn't so jealous.

School went well and believe it or not I didn't fall asleep in class. Last bell rings and I'm riding home with Nichelle. We head to the movies and her place afterwards. We looked at some videos, made up some dance routines and ate pizza. We planned to go shopping tomorrow. Not looking for anything in particular, maybe just see what all Summer stuff they got out. I tried on some of my shorts from last year and can't even button them. Deon mentioned my weight the last time we were together, but not in a bad way. He said my breasts were getting bigger and my hips were starting to spread. Of course, he felt like he should take the credit for it and said he liked it though. He may, but I'm sure not liking the scale. I've gained 7 lbs. over the last month. I guess it's because I been snacking more at night. Here lately every time, I sit down for a study session, I have to have my chips, cheese dip, and a drink close by.

    We make it to the mall and head straight to the food court. Sat in the atrium people watching. One of our favorite

things to do. This is a College town, so there are a lot of College students here today. I figure they are as up to date on fashion as possible, so we decide to try and get some ideas for the new Summer trend.

    Seems like all the girls are wearing tight stonewashed shorts, multi color t shirts with matching shoes. We head to

our favorite clothing store. Grabbed a few outfits and headed to the dressing rooms. They had all the styles we saw earlier.

We each got 5-6 outfits a piece. Nichelle looked amazing but I can't fit the outfits I picked out, so I got to go up to a size 1112. I been in a 9/10 for the last 3-4 years. By the time I try to find everything in the new size, I'm left with 1 outfit and a very bruised ego.

Jade: That's it. I been working out, but I've been messing up foodwise, so I'm going on a diet for real. I needed this wake-up

call.

Nichelle: You go right ahead. I got too much stress with this Semester, so I know I'm not going to be able to diet. Especially since me, stress eating, and procrastination have a love hate relationship. But hey it works for me every time.

Jade: Well good for you but it sure aint for me…

We head back to the food court to grab a bite to eat. I wasn't talking much because I'm really bothered about having to go up a size in Jeans. Nichelle is rambling on talking about the wet t-shirt contest/party she's going to. Of course, she said she wasn't going to enter but was going to be there in her daisy dukes, white t-shirt and neon green bra.

Nichelle: Girl what's wrong with you?

Jade: I'm just tripping about not being able to fit those outfits.

Nichelle: Aw girl its ok. Were about to be Seniors. We're all going to gain a few pounds because our body is changing. I know mine is and the guys love this body of mine, lol.

Nichelle had all kind of friends, but she doesn't have a boyfriend. She more of the round a way girl who's friends with all the guys. A few of them are interested in her but we both made a pact not to talk to anybody were friends with. I will admit, some of our guy friends are starting to look a lot better than they did back in the day. But neither one of us could see either one of them like that.

We get out our food and were both starving. Its 5:00 and we haven't eaten since like 9. Plus, with trying on all those clothes we have definitely worked up an appetite. I got some nachos and Nichelle got tacos. I ate one bite and could feel my stomach feeling queasy. I put the food down and pushed the plate to the other side of the table.

Nichelle: Jade girl, what you doing? I thought you were hungry.

Jade: Girl I don't know but that food, just smelling it got me feeling like I need to throw up.

Nichelle: Sounds like somebody needs to pee on a stick.

Jade: What?! Girl don't put that on me. I'm pretty sure it was the pizza. I ate some the other day and it made me throw up the next day. Then I'm feeling sick now and we ate some last night. I think I'm just starting to have issues with Pizza.   Nichelle: No ma'am honey, I'm not putting it on you Deon did!! lol
Jade: Shut up. It aint no way I could be pregnant.

Nichelle: Why not ? You and Deon been playing husband and wife for a while now.

Jade: Yea we have, but he pulls out every time. The only time he didn't was the first time and that was over a year ago. I know I've put on a few extra pounds but I aint no elephant. They are the ones pregnant for almost 2 years.

Nichelle: Jade. Now you know the pull-out method is the easiest way to get pregnant. That shit doesn't work. Why you think them people that practice the Rhythm method stay knocked up. But for real, you said, you been extra tired, sleeping more, snacking at night, put on a few pounds and you have been extra moody here lately.

Jade: Now don't you think if I was pregnant, I would know

Nichelle: Ok, when did you have your last period?

Jade: Last month around the 5th. No wait, it was the beginning of the month before, like the 5th

Nichelle: Okk so it's the 18th which means you should have already had 2 cycles since then.

Jade: Wait, I did have a cycle since then though. It was like 2 days and wasn't heavy, but it was a period.

Nichelle: Have you ever had a period like that?

Jade: No but I have been working out and I read that when you work out your cycles get off track.

Nichelle: Girl, I've saw you work out. You do, 3 sets of 10 sit ups and walk in place for 10 minutes. I hardly think that's enough exercise to jack your period up

Jade: Hey I do work up a sweat. But anyway, I'm not pregnant and to prove it to you I'm going to buy a test.

Nichelle: Please, do and take it as soon as possible and I want to be there when you do.

Jade: Of course, you will be right there because I can't wait to shut your mouth

I was so scared buying that test. Not because of what the results may be but because I just knew I was going to run into somebody I knew. You would have thought I was smuggling drugs the way I was speed walking to the register. We head to the car and as soon as I closed the door Nichelle told me to hand her the test. She read the instructions and it said its better to take it first thing in the morning.

Jade: Dang, I sure wanted to get it out the way.

Nichelle: Oh well, looks like we will get up extra early then

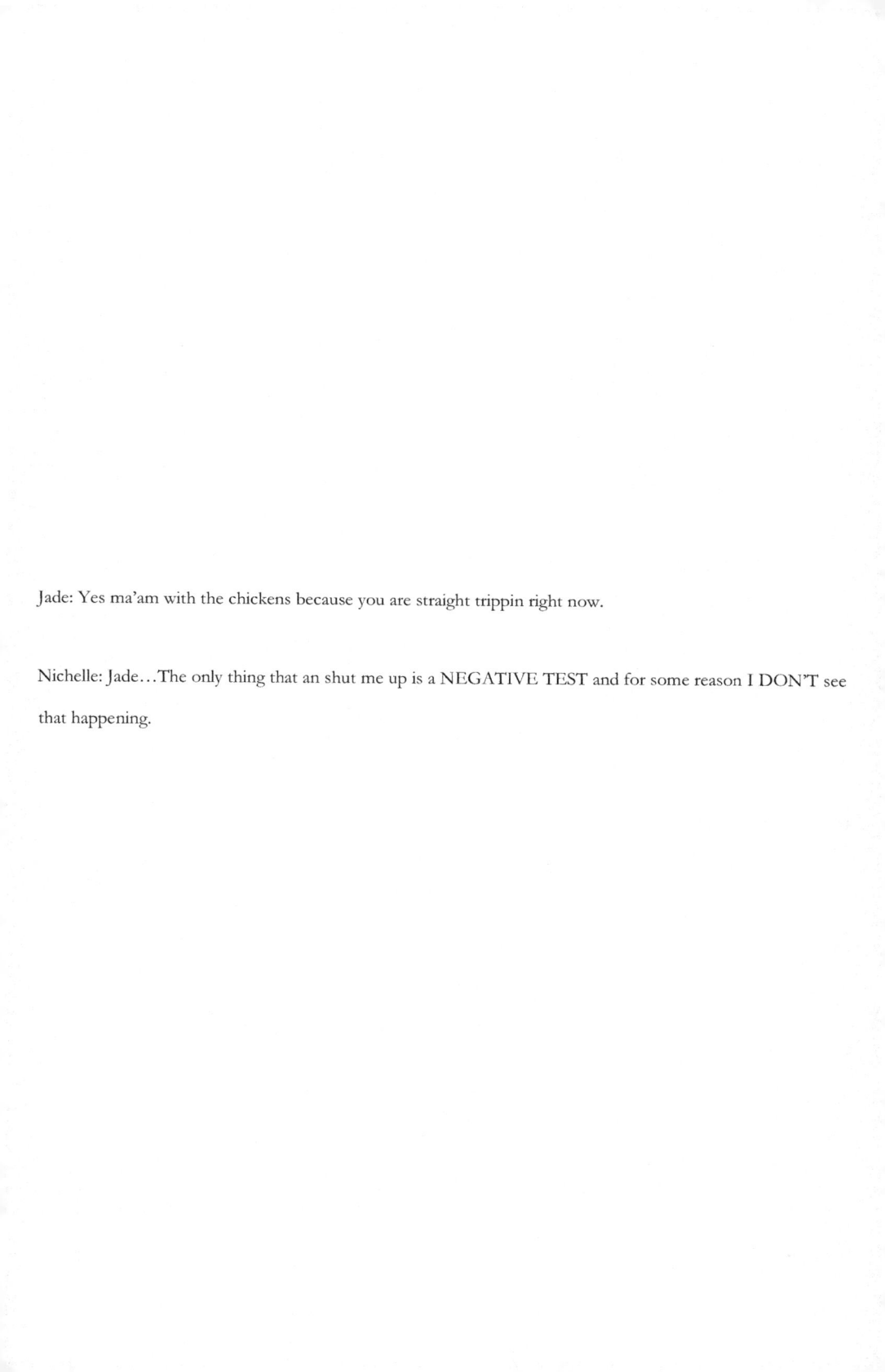

Jade: Yes ma'am with the chickens because you are straight trippin right now.

Nichelle: Jade…The only thing that an shut me up is a NEGATIVE TEST and for some reason I DON'T see that happening.

Pen to Paper

        Over the years, when nobody was looking, I would read information about adoption and how a lot of people who are adopted can grow up feeling abandoned. I guess all this talk about me needing to take a test has been making me think about it a little more about pregnancy and my birth Momma. I Try not to even let my mind go there because it gets frustrating to even think about. Who wants to think about being given away??

        The last article I read a week or so ago talked about how important it is to write or journal to cleanse the mind and soul. I decided to give it a shot and write a letter to my birth Momma. I tried several times to start the letter but kept putting the pen down because it almost felt pointless, silly, but on the other hand, it was overwhelming at the same time. That's crazy because the letter would never make it to her. For all, I know she may be dead by now. After a few tries, even though I had no idea how to start, it went something like this…

Hello__???_____,

This letter is not addressed to anyone in particular because I have no idea who you are. How crazy is that? The person who carried me inside them for nine months, I don't know. Do you even know me?? What do you know, if anything, about the family who raised me? Do you care? Have you tried to find me? Have you walked by people who may be around my age and wondered if they were yours? Was I made out of love? Were you made to get rid of me? Did you do something to lose me?

Part of me wants to be mad at you. The other part of me wants to thank you wholeheartedly.

Thank you because I have reimagined my life a million times about how things may have been different for me if I would have never been raised by Momma and Daddy. They loved me unconditionally and taught me the value of family, how to love, Loyalty, and hard work. How could you love me the way I have been by my family if you were ok with giving me away. You give away an unruly puppy or a piece of old broken furniture. Ironically for a long time, that's how I felt about myself— worn, less than, not worthy of love, and of no value.

Signed,

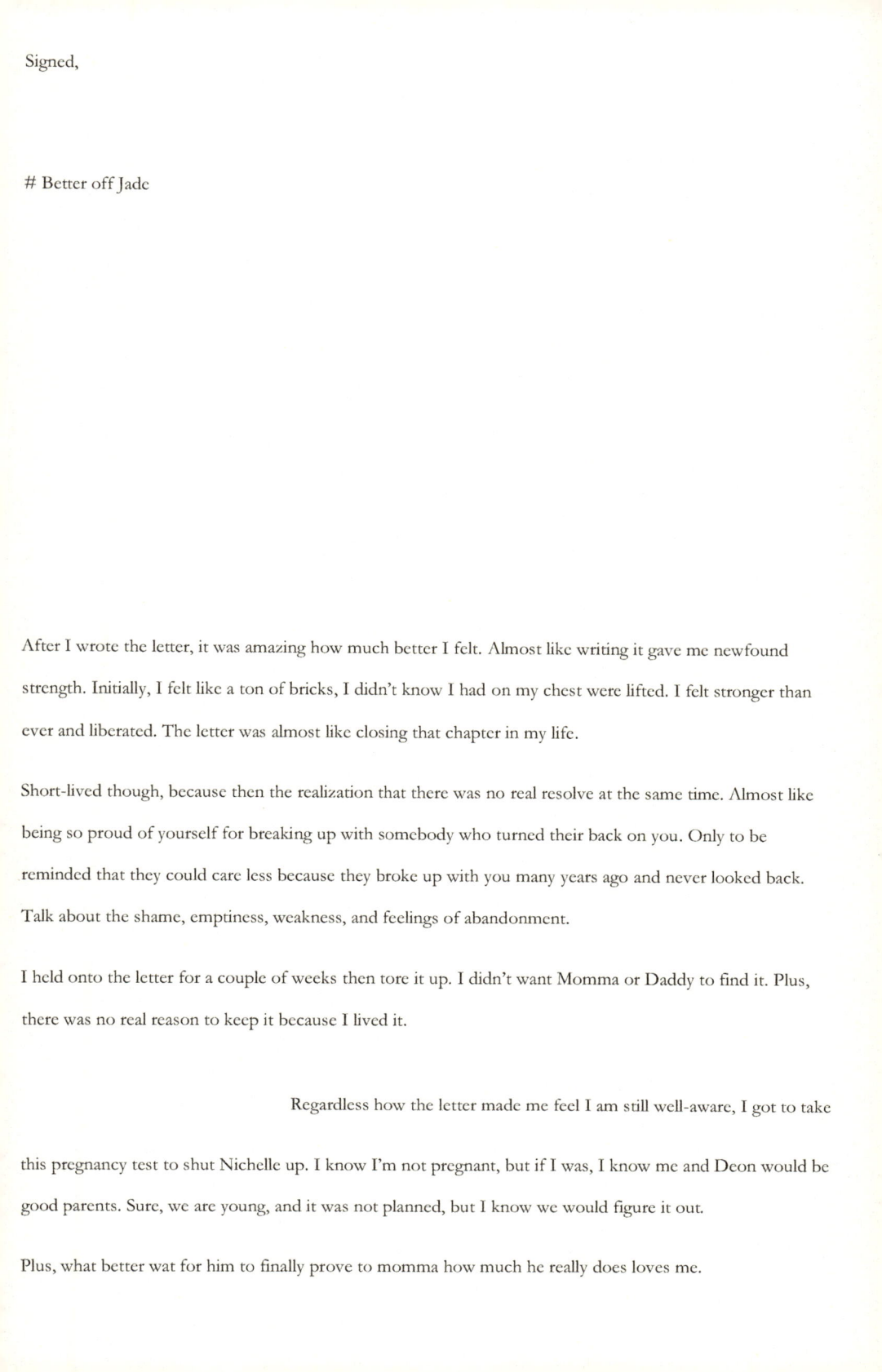

Better off Jade

After I wrote the letter, it was amazing how much better I felt. Almost like writing it gave me newfound strength. Initially, I felt like a ton of bricks, I didn't know I had on my chest were lifted. I felt stronger than ever and liberated. The letter was almost like closing that chapter in my life.

Short-lived though, because then the realization that there was no real resolve at the same time. Almost like being so proud of yourself for breaking up with somebody who turned their back on you. Only to be reminded that they could care less because they broke up with you many years ago and never looked back. Talk about the shame, emptiness, weakness, and feelings of abandonment.

I held onto the letter for a couple of weeks then tore it up. I didn't want Momma or Daddy to find it. Plus, there was no real reason to keep it because I lived it.

Regardless how the letter made me feel I am still well-aware, I got to take this pregnancy test to shut Nichelle up. I know I'm not pregnant, but if I was, I know me and Deon would be good parents. Sure, we are young, and it was not planned, but I know we would figure it out.

Plus, what better wat for him to finally prove to momma how much he really does loves me.

The End

Variations of Jade Book club chat

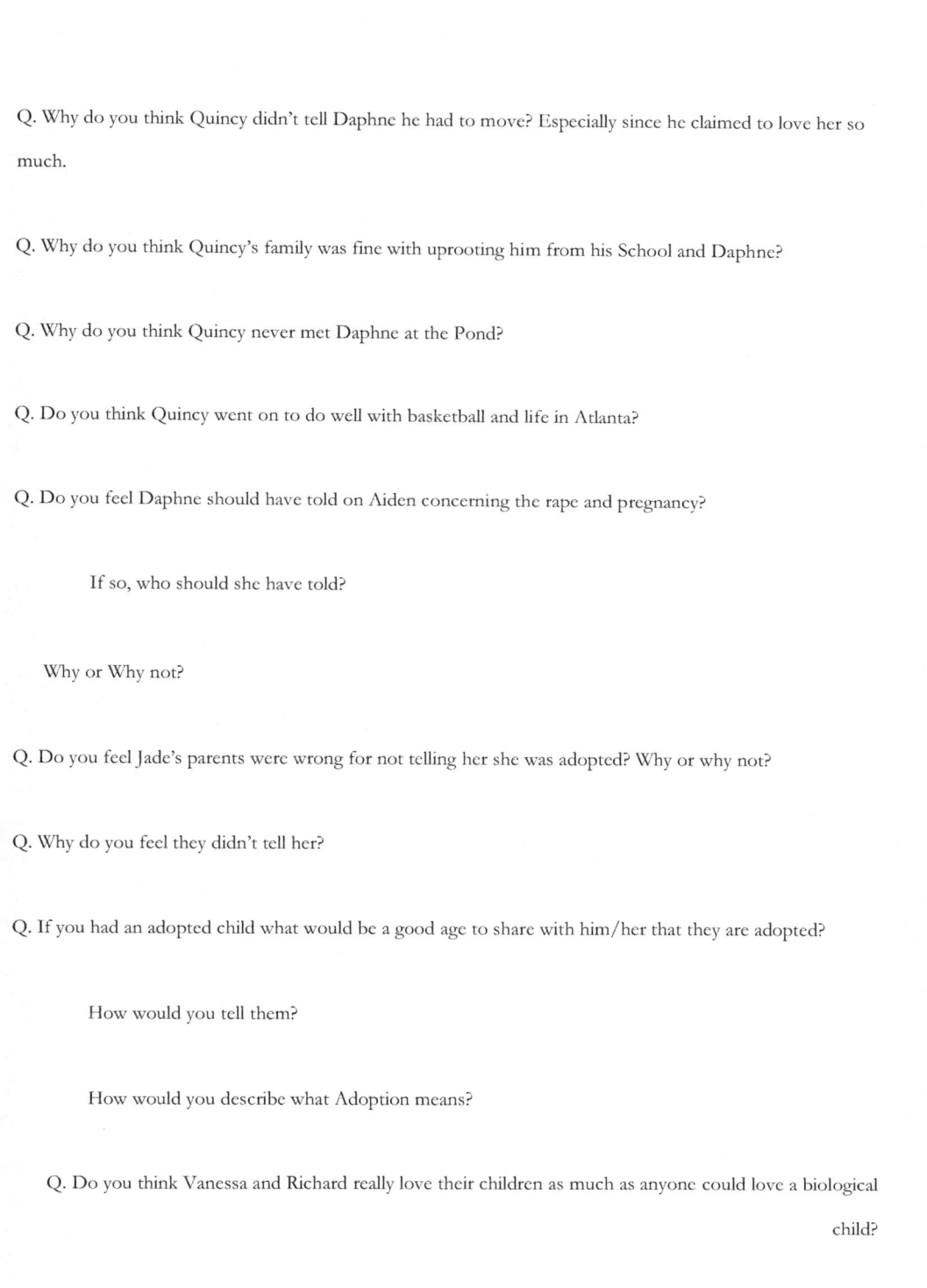

Q. Why do you think Quincy didn't tell Daphne he had to move? Especially since he claimed to love her so much.

Q. Why do you think Quincy's family was fine with uprooting him from his School and Daphne?

Q. Why do you think Quincy never met Daphne at the Pond?

Q. Do you think Quincy went on to do well with basketball and life in Atlanta?

Q. Do you feel Daphne should have told on Aiden concerning the rape and pregnancy?

    If so, who should she have told?

  Why or Why not?

Q. Do you feel Jade's parents were wrong for not telling her she was adopted? Why or why not?

Q. Why do you feel they didn't tell her?

Q. If you had an adopted child what would be a good age to share with him/her that they are adopted?

    How would you tell them?

    How would you describe what Adoption means?

    Q. Do you think Vanessa and Richard really love their children as much as anyone could love a biological child?

Why or why not?

Q. Do you think Jade is interested in finding her birth mother, and or father?

Q. If you were adopted, would you?

Q. What do you think will be the results of the Pregnancy test?

Q. Knowing what little you know about Jade and Deon, so far, do you think they will live happily ever after?

Note from the Mable

Hey all,

If you have just finished this book, I would like to WHOLEHEARTEDLY, say THANK YOU for your support. Especially since this is my first book, it sits very close to my heart that you decided even to give my book a chance ☺

The Variations of Jade Series is near and dear to me. Yes, I said SERIES…Call me crazy, but I'm not ready to be finished with Miss Jade yet...Please join my fan page to stay up to date, ask questions, or what have you.

Again, thank you for all your support!!!

Better off Jade

Book Description

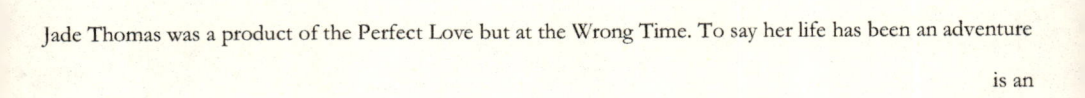

Jade Thomas was a product of the Perfect Love but at the Wrong Time. To say her life has been an adventure is an understatement. From the very beginning, she faced some very unique challenges, some ups, downs, and downs again. For as long as she could remember, for some reason, she felt like something was missing but could never put her finger on it. She believed in her heart; she never really had anyone to look at her. Well, at least not as he did. But even though that look was spell bounding, it came with events that have impacted her life in more ways than one. Follow Jade as she unveils many Variations of herself on her journey through heartaches, heartbreaks, and multiple life challenges with hopes of not only finding out what she's made of but WHO she is.

Made in the USA
Monee, IL
11 February 2021